The Christmas Dove

A Journey With The Christ Child

Carol Watson

Carol Watson

FIRST EDITION

Library of Congress Catalog Card Number: 96-83743

*Biblical Reference

ISBN 0-7880-0672-X PRINTED IN U.S.A.

This book is dedicated to

God

My husband, Jim

My children, Becky, Tim, and Michelle

Mom, Dad, Nana, Chris,
entire family and friends

All my students who dare
to dream, discover, dance, and believe

I

❄

She was alone. She was afraid. The injured white dove crawled into a secluded doorway of a cave-like stable. The warm smell of pungent straw, layered with animal sweat and well-worn leather, greeted her. The evening shadows crept across the stone walls and the stable sat quiet except for the drips of a watering trough and the squeak of a rusty hinge on a cobwebbed shutter. One lone manger, a storage bin, and a few barn tools peopled the room.

Dragging her limp wing to a large pile of clean straw, the dove quivered, burrowing under the prickly cover. She huddled, hurt and confused. Her thoughts drifted back through the day.

The dazzling sunrise had signaled a glorious day. High above the templed cities, the snow-white young dove played as free as the breath of God, heading for the lofty places of the dawning sky, feeling oneness with the swirling air currents.

The dove's interest turned to the throngs of people swarming into Bethlehem. She raced the centurion chariots and played tag among the brown-sandaled feet in the busy market place. The heat sent her to water buckets, quenching her thirst near wind-whipped robes of dark-eyed women who flapped her aside.

By afternoon the city bulged with travelers as the streets mounded with clutter. The dove ate the best spilt grain, squashed pomegranates, and bits of overripe dates. The dove's white beauty contrasted with the grime of the crowded city.

The bird fluttered to roost and preened herself, keeping out of the way of the smelly sheep. They bumped, bleated, and scuffed up the dust as if it had spread wings. The dove surveyed the people, animals, food, litter, noise, and smells. Crouching, she puffed herself, and dozed.

Creeping from a dusky alley, two boys flexed their slingshots on the white target. The dove never saw the rock. Her limp form plummeted helplessly to the ground, flopping in the dirt and pebbles. The bird lay panting, dazed, and gashed, her right wing bent with pain.

Looking for protection, she struggled in the path of evening traffic. Last minute vendors heading her way raced to beat the closing of the city gates.

Wheels grated inches from her. A foot absentmindedly kicked the dove off the pathway; she rolled like a dirty snowball down a hill into the stable where she now hid herself in the straw.

How could a day begin so joyously and end so troubled? Darkness closed around her like a black cloak. She tucked her head under her injured wing to rest and heal.

II

❄

That night a loud bang startled the dove. Eyes darting nervously, she remained still. Low voices and shuffling feet moved closer. A hoof stomped, a door slammed, and a lantern flickered eerily against the little manger where animals had nipped the wood. The straw, lifting above her, sent her heart pounding into her mangled wing. Struggling to move, but freezing, she looked up into the bearded face of a huge man.

Surprisingly, his eyes were warm. Gently he raised her against the long folds of his plain-cut robe, smelling of sawdust and perspiration, caressing her head with his calloused fingers. His lips, hidden in a bushy beard, curled into a smile. He spoke low and gently. "Well, little one, we need to share this stable with you." He quickly set the dove down, urgently piling straw into a larger bed.

The dove spied a young woman with a swollen stomach. Behind her stood a small donkey, sides swirled with sweat. The woman's dark eyes held concern. She shifted intensely, almost impatiently, watching the man's every move. Her fingers caressed her heaving sides. Laboriously she moved toward the bed of straw.

The man kneeled, spread out his coarse robe and helped her down, kissing her cheek. The dove's place was not far from the woman's head, and the bird gazed from the man to the woman as they spoke. "I'm sorry, Mary, it's the best I can do."

"Thank you, Joseph." She leaned against him, beads of cold sweat breaking on her forehead. "You had better go quickly. I am going to need a woman's help soon." She touched his stricken face. "Don't worry, I'll be all right. The pain has stopped for a while. Maybe I can get some rest."

Joseph looked grim but spoke encouragingly. "I will see if I can find a midwife in this crowded city. I won't be long. I promise."

"Joseph. Please hand me the small package attached to the donkey. Set it by my side. I've watched enough births to know what to do. There is a small caravan of people around a campfire in the field by the stable. Tell them I am about to give birth, and ask for some hot water. Bring it to me ... and please hurry."

Hesitantly Joseph rose to leave. He spied the dove nesting near his wife's head. He spoke nervously, "Keep her company, little one." Abruptly, he turned and left.

Shortly, Joseph reappeared and set steaming water in a wooden bucket next to Mary. He lowered himself, stroking her long black hair.

"I can't find a midwife," whispered Joseph. He slowly stood, running fingers through curly hair. "You know the ancient taboo; it is not fitting for a man to look upon a woman in childbirth." He placed his hand upon his hips, paused, and thoughtfully gazed at his wife. "But I won't leave you alone. I will stay with you." Mary reached up, caressed his hand, and brought it to her cheek. "Don't worry, Joseph, God understands."

The dove shifted herself in the straw, easing her sore wing. Rustling sounds made Mary and Joseph turn their heads. Mary's fingers shifted, touching the down of the dove. Quickly the hand drew back into a fist.

"Oh ... Joseph!" It came from between clenched teeth. "I think the time has come!"

Inexperienced as he was, Joseph knelt beside Mary, grasped her shoulders, and bowed his head.

A sacred light shimmered through a window, settling on the struggling husband and wife. A blazing star shone brightly over the stable.

Mary's hand flopped next to the bird and grasped the straw. Stretching out her small head, the dove touched the white knuckles. Instinctively, the dove released a low cooing song, cadences of one long note followed by two shorter notes. The bird watched tenseness come and go in the labored fingers. Slowly Mary's young face, glistening with sweat, turned and faced the dove. Eyes dilated, she focused and concentrated on the bird with all her might. The labor of life pressed down on her. Sensing her pain, and helping in the only way she knew, the bird continued her song of love, a slow, plaintive one-note chant. Suddenly, the bird stopped singing. She tilted her head to one side and then the other. Her eyes strained in the blinding light. She watched in wonder as Mary brought forth the beautiful baby.

Joseph moved forward, taking the child, lifting him for Mary to see. Together they marveled at him, his wholeness, infinitely small, pink, and perfectly formed. The baby uttered his first cry, a thrill to even God Himself.

Breathlessly, Mary directed Joseph, using the packet from the donkey and the hot water. The wiggling infant was quickly bathed, rubbed with salt, and wrapped in swaddling clothes. The straw bed was tidied.

Exhausted, Mary propped herself against a mound of straw to nurse the child. The dove, struggling with her bent wing, flicked the straw from her toes and teetered closer to the new mother and father.

Faces shone in proud wonder. Tears in his eyes, Joseph embraced the mother and child. As a seedling drawn to sunshine, the dove felt pulled into this circle of love. She nuzzled her downy head against Joseph's trembling fingers. Joseph picked up the dove and cradled her to his pounding chest. The dove cooed.

"His name is Jesus," said Joseph. And Mary added, "He will be great and will be called the Son of the Most High God. The Lord God will make Him a King and His kingdom will never end."*

The white dove felt one with this family: Mary, Joseph, and Jesus. It was a silent and holy night. The heavenly light billowed up and intensified on the small bed of straw. Far off, a majestic swell of angelic voices sounded.

III

❄

In the days following, the dove's loyalty to the baby grew. Except for occasionally exploring the musty corners of the stable, she remained faithfully roosted on the edge of the manger. Here the child slept and played. The dove cooed to the sleeping baby and entertained Him, prancing her white form back and forth like a peacock. Intently, Jesus' eyes followed her antics, answering with babbling and gurgling. Encouraged, the dove poked her velvet crown in and out of the straw, giving off noises. A bonding took place between the dove and the child.

As the sunset sank behind the purple hills, a warm breeze played with straw pieces on the stable floor. Wing healing, the dove hopped about on the stable floor eating discarded barley and oat seeds.

Outside, Joseph snapped twigs, piling them for the morning fire. Mary, kneeling on a pile of straw, leaned over Jesus who lay on a blanket. Dusting him with myrtle leaves, she sang softly:

> Low sweet baby,
> Gentle and mild,
> Born of flesh,
> But God's own Child,
> For to think,
> A Babe so small,
> Will change the world,
> And love us all.

Outside, the dove heard excited rumbling and rough voices. Mary questioningly looked to the dove and hurriedly wrapped a blanket around the baby, pressing Him tightly in her arms.

Joseph, unruffled, slipped through the crack in the door, stepping over to Mary. Leaning close to her, he whispered in her ear. Her expression changed, a secret smile now on her lips. Pausing, Joseph tenderly placed his finger into Jesus' small hand, the child grasping it securely. Then he turned and stepped outside into the shadows where low but ecstatic conversation resumed.

Shortly the door creaked open, spilling light into the room from the great star. Wings outstretched, the frightened dove moved backwards toward the manger. The silhouetted shadows moved closer.

Eyes darting, straining to see, the dove saw six earthy-looking men. Bronze, bushy-bearded, and wide-eyed, they closed in, staring. Sheepherders' hands clasped shepherds' staffs. Not a word was spoken. The bird pushed protectively against the hem of Mary's tunic. She whispered, "It's all right, little one. These shepherds learned of Jesus' birth and came to see Him." The dove, calmed at the words, nestled into the straw and watched.

Reverently the shepherds tiptoed closer on sandaled feet. With no sounds except for heavy breathing they laid down their wooden staffs, prostrating themselves for silent moments. Each bowed face reflected wonder.

Eventually, as silently as they crept in, the shepherds rose and backed out the stable door, suddenly chattering excitedly to Joseph. Words floated back to Mary: "Angels' voices ... heavenly choir ... Glory to God . . . ."

Sensing a tender moment, the dove fluttered to Mary's shoulder. The mother's cheek turned, brushing against the dove's silky feathers, feeling comfort. The realization of her child's destiny took hold of her. She whispered, "This is all so overwhelming." Tightly she pulled Jesus to her bosom.

The shepherds' soft voices floated into the night singing:

> "Glory to God in the highest ...
> And peace on earth ...
> Goodwill to all men . . . . "

IV

Late one night Mary and Joseph slept in the straw and Jesus murmured sweetly in His dreams in the manger; the dove dozed on the rim. A large pumpkin moon stared in the window. Suddenly a monstrous dog, yellow slanted eyes reflecting, jarred the stable door open, slithering inside. Ribs rippling, he prowled the dirt floor. Eyeing the sleeping baby and roosting dove, he licked hungry lips. Like a cobra ready to strike, swaying, he prepared to leap.

Sensing danger, the dove opened her eyes. Alarmed, she pierced a whistle. Immediately on his feet, seeing the dog, Joseph grabbed a broken two-pronged pitchfork. He maneuvered the struggling dog against a wall of straw, pinning him with the wooden prongs. With a free hand he roped a piece of leather around the dog's neck, securely tying him to a post.

Brushing his hands, Joseph turned to Mary, who rocked her wide-eyed baby and soothed the distraught dove.

"I think the ol' boy is starving. Look at those bones." Joseph went outside, returning in a few minutes, lugging a leaking bucket of slop.

"Here, boy! The swine in the back of the inn won't miss a little breakfast tomorrow morning. Help yourself." Greedily the massive head thrust itself into the bucket, stretching the leather leash taut, devouring the contents with powerful laps. "I don't think he will bother us now," reassured Joseph.

Mary tucked the sleeping baby in the manger, took her husband's hand, and led him back to the straw bed. They curled up once again for the night. From under the camel-hair blanket, a calloused hand reached to the manger rim, stroking the dove. "Thank you, friend." The dove puffed her feathers and cooed her song.

The dog's sides now bulged like a chipmunk's cheeks overstuffed with acorns and his glassy eyes beaconed the stable, as he looked hard and long at the contented sleeping family.

The light in the lantern flickered out. The dove, eyeing the brown mangy dog, finally went to sleep.

V

A rooster crowed, a trumpet sounded, and the dove's coos announced daybreak. The dog, still tied, but satisfied by food and rest, lay wide-eyed in the corner watching the dove and infant play. Mary and Joseph arose, beginning morning activities. Packing the donkey, Mary filled the water bag and wrapped morsels of barley cakes. Watching this new routine, the dove sensed something new for the day.

Bridling the donkey, Joseph strolled over to Mary who was washing utensils. Nearby, Jesus, kicking on a blanket, watched the dove. Joseph leaned over the child, clucking softly. Reaching up, the baby grabbed his beard, provoking a robust laugh from the carpenter.

"Well, son, today is a big event for you. Your mother and I are taking you to the Jerusalem temple to be dedicated to the Lord." Sliding an arm around Mary's waist, he said, "The morning's journey will be long and tiresome with the jostling crowds. We will return here this evening. Let's get an early start." Mary nodded, picking up Jesus.

After fastening his girdle, Joseph led the donkey, bulging with baggage, out of the stable into the crisp air and onto the dewy grass. Adjusting her mantle and securing Jesus in his swaddling wrap, Mary followed.

Joseph lifted them on the donkey. The dove flew out the stable door, landing on Joseph's shoulder.

"Well, little dove, let's see if you can keep up with us." Joseph waved the dove from his arm. The bird fluttered into the blue sky, circling around, glorying in the welcoming openness and almost forgotten freedom.

Joseph paused as if forgetting something, then slipped back into the stable. Cautiously he edged forward toward the dog who lay motionless, fearful. "Steady, boy. It's time you were on your way." Slowly, Joseph untied the leather binding, freeing the captive. Joseph raised a gentle hand, stroking the dog's head. The dog quivered, lifting bewildered eyes. "On your way, fella. Behave yourself." Joseph turned quickly and strode out the door. He grabbed the donkey, tugging forward. The holy family, with the white dove circling above, started their walk to Jerusalem.

Meanwhile, lurking behind, the mangy dog followed.

VI

The family wound out of the city into the hilly terrain of Bethlehem, sharing the road with vendor carts, squawking hens, soldiers on horseback, and bartering women.

The cobblestone street soon opened into a rocky road. The dove stretched her muscle-sore wings, soaring, dipping, and circling high above her new family.

Commanding a perfect view of their path behind and beyond, the dove delighted in this sun-filled day. The donkey, head down, plodded along, Joseph keeping the lead.

Soaring overhead, then coasting to a shoulder, the dove delighted Mary and Joseph in the game. It helped ease the burden of the day's journey.

Jesus alternated in first finding His dove, then napping in his mother's arms.

By mid-morning the heat intensified. The travelers, weary, stopped for rest and food. Under the shade of a fig tree Mary sat on a blanket changing and nursing the baby. The dove perched on a low dogwood tree above Mary's head. Joseph, across the road, with people pushing for room, watered the donkey. Busy talking, he did not notice danger inching toward his family. Out of the shadows a cobra slithered its four-foot form toward the nursing mother and child. Darting its forked tongue, it targeted closer and closer through the sand, deadly and silent. The serpent stopped short of the blanket, stiffening upward for a strike, spreading its neck in a menacing hood.

From above, the dove caught the movement, instantly letting loose her whistle. Forgetting her own safety, she swooped near the snake's pointed nose. The snake swayed for a strike, hissing at the bird.

Mary paled. Shielding the baby with her body, she knew better than to move. Fearfully she froze.

Instantly out of the bushes burst the mangy dog. The massive jaws clamped the snake from behind. The turbulence of dust and growling made a whirlpool of pebbles on the blanket, knocking the dove to one side. With expert precision, the attacker whiplashed the reptile, slamming it against the tree trunk again and again. The snake, hanging loose, dangled, eyes bulging. Lower lip trembling, Mary's eyes widened with relieved surprise. Amazed, she spoke to herself, "He must have followed us all morning." Triumphantly the dog paraded the dead snake in front of Mary and Jesus, seeking recognition. He desperately wanted this family's acceptance. The dove, still defensive, flapped her wings.

Joseph, on hearing the commotion, dashed across the road, accompanied by a Roman centurion he had befriended at the well. The young soldier, having untied his whip from his belt, poised it to strike the dog. Joseph's hand spread back against the soldier's chest, halting him. The dust settled. The dog dropped the dead snake at Joseph's feet. Joseph's panicky eyes raced over Mary and Jesus. "Are you all right?" he asked. Mary took a deep breath, forcing a nod. Then, patting her knee, she said, "Come here, fella."

Hungry for a soft touch, the dog, whimpering, crawled on his belly to the mother and child. The baby, alert to something new, reached out and grabbed the dog's matted hair. Mary soothingly lay her hand on him. The dog, still crouching, thumped his skinny tail in joy. Feeling neglected, the dove flew to Mary's shoulder.

Stunned at the dog's devoted behavior, Joseph stood transfixed, looking from the dog to the dead snake. He too rewarded the dog with a ruffled tussle. Good-naturedly he slapped the centurion on the shoulder. "Well, what do you know? I guess we now have a dove to watch from above and a dog to protect from the ground. We've earned a rest and I'm hungry. Maximus, will you join us for lunch?"

Never turning down a free offer, the soldier grinned. Removing his helmet, the burly man revealed a young face, brown beard, hazel eyes. He stepped across the road to the watering trough, quickly returning with his dapple horse. Snorting water from nostrils, the horse rubbed his head against his master's shoulder, almost unbalancing him. Maximus laughed, briskly scratching the velvet nose.

Joseph carefully watched the young man. Under his authoritative appearance, Joseph figured him a friendly man with a keen sense of adventure, a zest for life. Firm lines set around fine lips. He had the brow of a dreamer but the mouth of a soldier, and appeared a man of sensitive feelings but inflexible will.

Normally a Jewish carpenter from Galilee and a Roman soldier in Caesar's army would go their separate ways, but both took an immediate liking to the other while watering their animals. The soldier tied his horse to a tree, while Joseph helped

Mary spread their scant meal of barley cakes, cheese, and assorted dried fruit.

Jesus kicked and stretched on a blanket, entertaining the dove and the mangy dog. Mary, Joseph, and the young soldier stretched out on a grassy knoll, eating the noon meal.

After the meal, Mary napped with Jesus, while the men sprawled on the ground, backs against boulders, talking.

Maximus picked his teeth with a stick. "The peasantry have alerted us to a strange caravan from the East heading this way. Three kings, star gazers of a sort. Their path meanders as if they're not sure of their destination."

Maximus leaned forward, lowering his voice. "The people in my district are uneasy at the strange glowing in the sky for the past five weeks. Who knows, maybe that's what the kings are seeking. Nevertheless, there's a reporting of eerie restlessness of animals, while shepherds on Jericho Hills are spreading tales about strange happenings."

Joseph listened keenly, then changed the subject with information about the crowded conditions of Bethlehem during the census.

"Mary and I hoped to room with relatives, but with the city being crowded, we couldn't locate them. The inns were full. With Mary's birthing time, we were lucky to find a stable to stay in temporarily." Joseph idled a few moments drawing symbols in the dirt with his finger, contemplating what Maximus would think if he knew the truth about Jesus. In spite of this new friendship, Joseph decided to keep his thoughts to himself, reflecting on what Maximus said without comment.

Nearby Jesus broke the silence with comical gurgling noises which distracted the men. Mary arose, propping Jesus on her hip.

"You have a beautiful family, Joseph. There is something very special about that boy of yours. He has the most remarkable eyes I've ever seen." Maximus reached for the baby. Taking him, he swung Jesus high over his head. The baby laughed. "Yes sir, son, you definitely are a father's prize."

Maximus placed the child on the blanket, pulled a gold bracelet from his girdle and gave it to Jesus, whose small hand clasped the ringlet, putting it into his mouth.

The sun's reflection on the circle resembled a halo framing the baby's face. "Thank you, Maximus," Mary said. She picked up the bracelet. "You are too generous." She tried to hand it back, but Maximus had turned to untether his horse.

Having said he delayed too long, Maximus thanked Mary for the lunch. He firmly clasped hands with Joseph, mounted his pawing horse and waved farewell to this loving family journeying from Bethlehem.

VII

❄

The sun spewed its hot breath as the Holy Family approached Jerusalem, brimming with sweat and noise. Shouting drivers cursed, donkeys brayed, sheep bleated, and pigs squealed. The poor cried for bread. Lepers and outcasts slithered in and out of shadows like forbidden thoughts. Rich Greeks rode in sedan chairs, the servants shouldering the yokes easily, walking steadily. Musicians and children danced in the street while zealots and harlots glared coldly at each other. Guards, on magnificent horses, wound among the crowds, trying to keep a semblance of order in this carnival of activity.

The dove, flying above the crowds, concentrated on overseeing. In contrast, the mangy dog dragged along like a discarded mop, snatching tidbits that fell from vendors' wagons or lapping gritty rainwater from the gutter. The vagabond defied anyone to harm his wards. He snarled at a beggar daring to approach the mother and child on the donkey.

The dove rose to the highest pinnacle of the city gate. From this summit, joining hundreds of pigeons and doves perching and fluttering in swarms, the dove watched Mary and Joseph weave among the pushing crowds. Occasionally Mary shielded her eyes, scanning the walls for their dove. The dove, seeing the gesture, flew down, circling. Mary in return smiled and the dove returned to her roost. The mangy dog kept close to the donkey, wagging his tail at the dove's game.

A stout soldier on a wide-eyed mare moved the crowd back with a whip. "Stand back, swine!" he growled. "Kings of the East are passing through! Herod is waiting for his guests. Make way!" Crack! The whip lashed and people spread like waves receding on the sand. Joseph kept back. He stretched to see like everyone else but kept an arm protecting Mary and Jesus. The whip often caught the front row. Mangy dog huddled to Joseph's side, peeking out around his legs; he knew the feel of a whip too well. Joseph turned to Mary who slid off the donkey.

"This must be the caravan of kings of which Maximus spoke." A wave of excitement washed over the crowd, all craning their necks. Three magnificent camels strutted loping walks, each carrying a royal king. The camels, haughty noses in the air, were dressed in the finest wrappings gold could buy.

The kings' velveteen robes of magenta, lavender, and gold billowed out like puffballs over the dromedary humps. The majestic figures topped themselves with spectacular headpieces. Sparkling rings covered every finger, while beaded girdles bulged money bags. Massive golden collars around their necks marked them as Parthian nobles and the winged circles of gold resting upon their breasts were the sign of the priesthood of the Magi. The kings smiled, one black skinned, and two fair, the last man looking considerably older.

Three servants riding smaller and less decorated beasts traveled behind each king. Their camels carried the necessities: tenting, baskets of food, clothing, and gifts. Each servant wore an ivory-handled sword against his thigh.

The procession moved directly by Mary, Jesus, and Joseph. The lead king, looking perplexed, stopped short, held up his hand, and reined in his camel, as he looked for someone or something. His eyes scanned the crowd.

The soldier, fidgeting with the whip, rode over, politely saying, "Your Majesties, it would be wise to keep moving. I don't know how much longer I can hold this crowd." The first king shrugged, tapped the growling camel on the neck with a jeweled leather crop, and continued toward the palace.

After the kings passed, the peasants flowed back like whitecaps on the shore. The pageantry enchanted Mary. But now she was hot and tired and wanted to get to the temple as quickly as possible. She mounted the donkey. Joseph tugged the beast forward.

The sun turned west, gleaming into sparkles that danced off the temple gates. Near a stone wall Joseph took the dove to his finger. "Wait here for us. We'll look for you when we return. Keep where we can spot you." Chuckling, he continued, "Even though white doves are everywhere, I would recognize you among hundreds." Mary nodded. "Now don't get lost. Jesus won't sleep tonight without you on his manger."

Jesus reached an outstretched hand to the bird. The bird recognized the gesture, nuzzled the baby's shoulder with her head, and flapped her wings. She flew off, circling high and wide.

Joseph ordered the mangy dog to stay in a dusty corner of an outer gate. Then Mary, Joseph, and Jesus disappeared behind the temple gates.

VIII

❄

The mangy dog lumped himself in a dusty corner against a wooden crate, one eye watching the dove. Across the street, joining six other birds, the dove roosted on a wooden beam over a tannery. A vegetable vendor tossed dehydrated lettuce and wilted carrots in the gutter. Two young urchins grabbed the garbage like treasures in their arms and scurried into a doorway.

Shortly a greasy, fat man, pushing a slatted box on wheels, appeared. Around the man's bulging belly hung a key. He breathed heavily, rings of sweat layered under his double chin. Wiping his forehead with a soiled cloth, his eyes roved the street, finally resting on the tannery. Tongue licking his swollen lips, he picked up a large net on a stick along with a grain bag. He lumbered over, sprinkling grain on the cobblestones beneath the chattering doves, then silently moved back into hiding. The scar over his eye twitched. He waited and watched.

The doves eventually spied the treat. Greediness led them to the trap, Jesus' dove included. They pecked busily, stuffing their gullets. Without warning, the net slammed over four birds. The captor aimed for the white ones, the prizes which brought the best prices from the temple priests.

The dove felt the weight of the snare push her on the stones. She fought to escape but tangled more in the netting. Two birds escaped, creating a flapping frenzy. People passed by, only glancing at the fray. Plucked from the entangled heap, a filthy hand squeezed the dove's breast. She recoiled.

"Here's a white beauty," the voice rasped. The man thrust her into an odorous box stuffed with doves of assorted sizes and shades. Swollen fingers locked the doorlatch, while birds frightened in the murky prison squawked and pecked. The box lifted, jostled, and slid the birds around like loose coins in a pocket. Dark clouds gathered on the horizon while the fat man wheeled his feathered captives down a desolate sidewalk. The path led to a small ornamental gate behind the temple. The man, impatient, pulled a rope from a bell protruding from the door frame. He waited. A dog barked.

Presently a servant, turbaned and robed, opened the gate. Without a word he pressed a sack of coins into the fat man's palm, dragged the cage through the doorway, and slammed the gate shut.

The fat man turned into the face of the mangy dog. Snarling, the dog eyed the money sack. Leaping at the man's wrist, he set his teeth into the tattered sleeve, giving the arm a sharp shake, sending the bag flying. The dog stood ferocious, and barked, growled, and snapped at his victim. The man fled as if Hades' three-headed watchdog had appeared.

Yellowed teeth picked up the bag of coins and placed them into low bushes near a rock fence. A small lizard sprawled on a boulder, the only witness.

Loping toward the gate, the dog found and dug under the bottom rung. Dirt flew like a mini sandstorm. He squirmed his massive body through the hole, shook himself, and slinked into a blackened culvert in the stone wall. He looked for the dove.

The dove bumped, banged, and slid inside the wooden cage. Eventually a servant rested it on a marble bench in the temple's outer courtyard. Tables laden with merchandise lined the bazaar-like atmosphere. Worshippers afforded offerings according to their wealth. Moneychangers shrilly explained the larger the sacrifices the more blessings earned. Consequently business flourished; worshippers, travelers, and tourists milled everywhere.

Behind the bird cages limped a scrawny man with a prickly beard and fuzzy mustache. A temple cap, Kippah, crushed his bushy hair outward. A striped tallith, or prayer shawl, draped his yellowed robe. The temple claimed him on the lowest rank.

Into the cage he plunged his bony hand, inspecting the merchandise. The ill fingers grasped the dove, lifting her out of the squawking pandemonium. Feathers flew everywhere. The man inspected her plump body, saying, "Yes ... fine." He thrust her above his head shouting, "Sacrifices for the temple! This one pleases God." People turned their heads and looked. Animals screamed within the temple's inner court. Obnoxious smells of incense mixed with burnt animal flesh permeated the air.

High above the seller's head the dove saw Mary and Joseph sauntering through the crowd. The dove whistled, but lutes and timbrels struck up a concert, muffling her cries. Mary, Joseph, and Jesus vanished in the activity.

A rabbi, shuffling his feet and carrying a Torah, stepped up. Impatiently he placed coins into the moneychanger's hand and mumbled, "This should take care of my offering today." The seller stuffed the dove into a square stick holder and slammed the lid. The rabbi, muttering to himself, took the dove and hobbled toward the sacrificial altars.

Breezes stirred Mary's mantle as dark clouds veiled the western hills. A trumpet sounded announcing services while temple attendants swung open the gates. Bells tinkled.

The inner court, dotted with sacrificial altars, yielded a solemn atmosphere. Numerous circular stone platforms, filled with coals and surrounded by steps, dominated the area. Blood stained the outside stones, while lambs' wool, feathers, and excrement fouled the ground. Slaves in white tunics attended the sacrifices.

Mary and Joseph, filing by, refused to look, but lent sorrowful listening to the animal cries. With bloody hands an attendant tied a lamb's legs, slit its throat, red gushing, heaving it to the crimson eyes of the coals. Another attendant ran skewers through live birds, propping them in rows over the fires. The roasted meats fed the rabbis, sadducees, and pharisees. Offerings stood stored along stone walls, as needed for the temple meals.

People crowding in the gate filed past a stubby priest sitting at a table. Each individual or family, after presenting an offering, received a blessing. Lamb offerings brought longer blessings, while the pigeon offerings brought the shortest. The old rabbi, five people ahead of Mary and Joseph, set the dove on the table. The priest gave a blessing to the rabbi. A slave stepped forward, snatched the dove's cage, and stacked her among the other bird cages. The dove tried to whistle but couldn't.

Mary and Joseph stepped forward. Mary lowered her eyes as Joseph placed their doves on the table. Without looking up, the priest chanted, "May you who are here be blessed in the name of the Lord. We bless you from this house of the Lord.

May He who is supreme in power, blessing, and glory bless this man, woman, and child." In the same breath he said, "God's blessing to you," impatiently motioning toward the temple. Mary and Joseph responded, "Amen and God be with you also." They moved toward the temple door.

Suddenly Mary stopped, tilted her head, and listened. At the same time, Jesus awoke from a nap and climbed his mother's shoulder, peeking wide-eyed at the stacked bird cages.

"Joseph! Something is wrong," Mary said. Just then the sky opened her portals, drenching the court. Wind whipped the altar fires. A hissing voice rose as water droplets beat on red coals. A rumbling clap sent people scurrying like locusts in a field fire. Mary and Joseph, bodies bent over Jesus, ran toward the cages where a dormer sheltered the stinging rain.

The dove, seeing them, forced her distress call. Her pitiful cry rang clear. Joseph turned his head toward the sound, recognizing the whistle. Mary also saw and knew. She grabbed Joseph's hand as a crack of lightning, followed by a thunderous rumble, quivered the temple walls.

Nearby, the mangy dog bolted from the shadows, bumping people, overturning tables, adding to the disruption of the storm. Temple guards chased the dog while the wind howled, lightning flashed, and people scattered.

Into the inner court he careened, ribs heaving, tongue hanging, and mouth foaming. He collided broadside of the stacked cages with his shoulder. Cages were overturned, breaking, bouncing, and banging in every direction. Doves broke out, shrilling cries of surprise, releasing a billowing flutter of whiteness.

A white dove broke forth, circled down, and perched on Mary's shoulder. Hands eagerly stroked her. The bird rose again and took flight.

Simultaneously Mary and Joseph looked upward, smiling. Meanwhile, guards rummaged through empty bird cages, arguing among themselves.

A dark form inched from shadows behind, pressing a cold nose into Joseph's hand. Without drawing attention to himself Joseph patted the panting head. Content filled the dog. He crouched low, crawled on his belly, and hid behind rubbish. Winding their way around cages and rain-soaked people, the holy couple entered the temple to dedicate their firstborn son to God.

X

Jesus' service stirred a fervor in the temple when an old man, Simeon, acknowledged Jesus as the promised Messiah. A holy woman, Anna, the prophetess, came out of a crowd and ackowledged the Child also. As Mary and Joseph descended the temple steps, liberated doves perched everywhere. Cooing the good news, they filled the city with nature's concert. People heard birds singing in every corner of the city that afternoon and talked about the phenomenon for years.

Joseph picked up the donkey at the hitching post as the dove circled above. The celebration of joy continued as they went out from the temple and down the road leading from Jerusalem where the mangy dog triumphantly joined them, tail wagging and tongue lolling. Mangy dog puzzled Joseph when he dropped a soiled bag of coins at his feet. Joseph's comment was, "Only God knows where you found this." Taking the bag, Joseph gave the coins to the the poor crying for bread. If dogs could smile, the mangy dog would have been doing so, while closely trotting at Joseph's side.

Tired but happy, they continued their journey back to the stable in the City of David.

XI

The moon rose, giving cue to the locust song. Mary and Joseph relaxed in the stable after the return journey to Bethlehem. Outside, the dove, circling the area, saw visitors approaching. Landing on an olive branch she looked closer. Near the stable stood the caravan of kings that had caused the excitement in Jerusalem.

The sun sank low and framed the three kings in glowing tapestry, their jewels sparkling. "The point of light stops here," one said.

The dove watched as silent minutes passsed. The kings sat motionless upon camels, heads looking skyward. The oldest of the kings lowered his gaze. His eyes squinted, then widened. Shaking his crop, he burst out. "There it is! The sign! It's the sign in my vision!" He pointed a quivering finger at the dove. All heads turned to look. Some unknown force held the dove firmly in place under the blinding light, yet she did not feel afraid.

"In my vision, the star's brilliant tail pointed directly down on the child's birthplace where a white dove sat in an olive tree. This is it! We are here!" A silence followed. The kings looked around, questioning what to do next.

Just then Joseph came out of the stable, having heard the disruption. The dove flew to Joseph's shoulder, unaware that this gesture had also been envisioned in the wiseman's dream. The wisemen tapped their camels with riding sticks, commanding the camels to drop. Servants ran forward, dismounting the men. Each king walked toward Joseph, bending reverently on one knee. Jewelry jangled in the silence.

Joseph recognized the kings who had ridden through Jerusalem. His knees felt unsteady and he stood speechless. These kings bowed before him, a mere carpenter from Nazareth. The dove's toes grasped his shoulder, jogging Joseph's memory back to his boyhood when the firm hand of his father gripped his shoulder, keeping him silent in awkward moments.

The dark-skinned king arose, followed by the others. He spoke with a distinct accent, from very pink lips. "Whom do we have the honor of addressing?"

"I am Joseph of Nazareth, the house of David," Joseph replied. The king, aware of Joseph's discomfort, laid a comforting hand on his shoulder, asking, "Is there a newborn child here?"

Joseph answered, pointing to the stable door. "Yes, my wife Mary is inside with her newborn son, Jesus."

With amazed looks, the kings' composure broke, exploding into jovial pats and sighs of delight. The dove, still perched on Joseph's shoulder, bobbed her head and joined in the joy.

The first king turned suddenly. "Joseph, please. We beg your forgiveness for being rude. I am Caspar, this is Melchior, and here is Balthasar. We are Magi of the eastern countries, and we have traveled many days seeking the Messiah. We are visionaries and astrologers of a religious order, who believe the sign of this special star is according to prophecy. This prophecy promises a great star will appear at the birth of a child out of Bethlehem, who will become the Savior of Men.

"This divination was given five hundred years ago to Balaam, the son of Beor, the first of the Magi, and to each generation since. Now at last it appears to us. Living in different areas of Persia and Chaldea, each of us visioned the Christ Child's birth. We met to follow the star and search for this holy child to worship Him. Today, this prophecy is fulfilled!"

Joseph, astonished at this revelation concerning Jesus, meekly answered, "You are welcome to stay as long as you like. I apologize for the stable. We are here temporarily, the city being crowded because of the census."

Joseph motioned toward the door. Melchior pulled the door open. Inside, at the farthest corner, resplendent with starlight, they beheld Mary and the baby, looking exactly like the Virgin and Child in their visions. Mary, not seeing them, head bent, sang a lullaby. The kings, in awe, didn't move, each to his own in this magical moment.

Carefully, they closed the door. The kings' faces radiated joy and enchantment. Rubbing his hands excitedly, Melchior said, "First we will give instructions to set camp, then we will prepare ourselves according to custom for the adoration ceremony." Caspar walked to Joseph and embraced him. Clapping his hands together, Melchior ordered the servant to pitch tents. Caspar and Melchior hurried off, having so much to do in so little time.

XII

❄

At the stable, Joseph explained to Mary the circumstances of the kings' arrival. She marveled that these men had come so far to adore Jesus, then turned to a festive mood after hearing the kings' plans for the evening. After tidying up the stable, she bathed Jesus, then changed her mantle to the blue one given by her mother for her wedding.

The dove joined in the excitement. She fluttered about, getting in the way, preening herself while Jesus watched.

Meanwhile, Joseph took gifts from the kings to the innkeeper. The generous offerings more than paid for the use of his property. The innkeeper relished the esteem and publicity that the caravan brought to his inn. Secretly, he regretted not having room to lodge Joseph inside the inn.

Later that evening the kings emerged from their tents, wearing mantles of yellow, purple, and red silks. A servant carrying gifts accompanied each king.

The cortege paraded to the stable. Two servants entered, laid a cranberry carpet to the manger, and withdrew to a corner. Mary sat wide-eyed, holding Jesus on her lap near the manger. Joseph stood nearby. Mangy dog crawled to a corner, and dove perched cordially on the side of the manger.

All anticipated the kings' ceremony. The dream of Abraham was about to be played out. Caspar entered first. Mary sat straight and propped the infant on her lap. The child smiled, extending His arms. Caspar, bowing his head and crossing his hands to his breast, fell on his knees before the child. He unfastened a bag from his girdle, withdrawing handfuls of gold bars, each a finger length, thick and heavy. He lay them at Mary's feet. Mary lowered her eyes, nodding gratitude. Caspar backed away.

Next Melchior entered the door carrying a large ruby censer filled with greenish grains of resin, a gift of frankencense. He placed his gift at Mary's feet and knelt in adoration. He too then backed away.

Balthasar, arms full, took his time hobbling to the manger. He could not kneel, being too old and portly. Breathing hard, he unfolded a small table and placed upon it a golden vessel holding a delicate plant. The myrrh was a miniature bush with dainty white flowers. Magi are physicians as well as astrologers. Potent and expensive remedies such as myrrh are high on the list of favored treasures. The giving of myrrh is an insurance to good health. Balthasar bowed from the waist for a long time until Jesus gurgled. Lifting his head, he stepped back. In conclusion to the ceremony, the dove sang her love song, a low, plaintive melody. This lilting serenade brought tears to the kings' eyes, their joy complete.

After the ceremony, people drifted outside. Mary talked with the kings; each in turn held the baby and marveled at His beauty.

The feast after the adoration ceremony was the finest seen in Bethlehem.

The kings, Mary, Joseph, and Jesus were entertained upon piles of colored pillows inside a yellow cone-shaped tent. Platters of duck, fish, kid, cheeses, honey bread, olives, dates, and fig cakes were laid before the honored guests on low tables. Wine and goat's milk bubbled in silver goblets. A dark-skinned boy of twelve sat crosslegged in the corner playing a haunting tune on a black ivory flute. Gentle breezes rippled against the walls of the tent as if keeping time to the music.

Flickering torches lit the Holy Child's face; the kings couldn't keep their eyes from Him, etching the face in their memories. Conversation stayed casual until the meal was over. Mary thanked her hosts for everything. As was custom, she excused herself with Jesus, leaving the men to talk. She was tired and it was late. With a nod from Caspar, two servants escorted her and the child back to the stable. As etiquette required, Joseph remained seated. The festive mood changed to one more somber.

Caspar spoke first. "Joseph, our love and joy in the past few hours far surpasses anything we have ever known. We didn't want anything to interfere in the adoration ceremony and festival. Now we want to speak privately about an urgent matter." Joseph looked questioningly.

Caspar continued. "Let me explain. We randomly followed the star and it led us to Jerusalem. There we halted because it became invisible. We took this as a sign that the Christ Child must be near so we stopped and inquired about the holy birth with the townspeople. We thought to see feasting and celebrating. We found nothing. There were no clues of the birth of a holy child.

"King Herod heard of our caravan and sent messengers to inquire about us. We learned the messengers went back to Herod and reported. He quickly gathered priests, scribes, and aged Jews to verify it in the scriptures. He led them to the palace rooftop to look for this great star we claimed to follow; they didn't see it. He believed at this point that we were just a hoax. The scribes and priests, holding back and afraid of Herod's wrath, assured Herod that there was nothing to our claim.

"We slept little in Jerusalem that night. Not knowing what to do next, we thought if anyone knew of this great happening, surely King Herod would know. We sent a servant to request a visit with him. He summoned us. We made a grand entrance through Jerusalem to the palace."

Reflecting, Joseph sipped his wine. "Yes, we saw your parade. Mary was especially enthralled with you." Balthasar jerked up his head. "I remember where you were for I stopped my camel, feeling the child's presence near me. Eh?" He smiled secretly, rubbing his gray beard. Pointing a gnarled finger at Joseph, he continued on. "It happened at the back of the city near the gate to Mount Calvary near a fish market." Joseph nodded. Balthasar continued. "I knew it! I did not think my faculties were leading me astray. Anyway, the soldiers pressed us to keep moving."

Melchior continued his story. "Guards ushered us into the palace. We demanded to know where the holy child might be since the great star disappeared at Jerusalem. Herod denied knowing of such a child. Finally he called his top scribe and questioned him at length. The scribe finally admitted that they found a passage in the holy book that foretold a holy child to be born in Bethlehem.

"Herod said, 'Go find this Messiah of the Jews in Bethlehem. After you pay homage to Him, return to Jerusalem and tell me where to find him so I may worship Him also.' We felt uneasy, but we promised King Herod we would honor his wishes."

Caspar went on. "It was late that night when we left King Herod's palace. We still couldn't find the star, although we will never understand the absence of the star at this point. Camping outside Bethlehem last night, we found the star again."

There was a moment of hesitation when the wisemen searched each other's faces. Caspar stood and spoke compassionately as he looked at Joseph. "Last night we all had the same dream. The message was clear. Herod deceived us. We should escape as soon as possible, for Herod plans our arrest when we return to Jerusalem, and when he locates Jesus, he will kill Him."

Joseph sucked in his breath. His mind blurred and his hands iced. A band tightened around his throat. Thoughts raced through his mind. *"Kill a baby? God's child? Flee! Get going! But we can't go back to Nazareth. Herod will find us. My family is known there. We need to escape far away... but where should we go? How can I tell Mary she can't go home?"*

Melchior placed a gentle hand upon Joseph's arm and spoke low. "We are leaving the first thing in the morning. Herod's soldiers, even now, are entering the city. Please go with us. We could take you and your family to Persia with us where we'd proudly raise the boy."

Numbly, Joseph sat trying to think reasonably. The offer to leave with the kings seemed the best solution.

Joseph said, "It may be God's will that I go with you but I need more time to pray, think this out, and verify my decision. In any case, I will be packed and ready to escape the city soon."

Joseph stood up. A servant helped Balthasar up and he moved stiffly to Joseph's side. Tears welled in his eyes. "If we hadn't given information to King Herod, you wouldn't be in this predicament. We are sorry." Balthasar broke down and wept.

Joseph put a firm hand upon his friend's shoulder and mounted courage to say, "God will be with us, friend." Joseph clasped arms with Caspar and Melchior, saying, "If God wills it, we will leave with you tomorrow. God be with you."

Balthasar teetered forward and embraced Joseph somberly, half whispering, "And God be with you also, my son." The carpenter turned and left the tent.

XIV

❄

Joseph threaded his way down an obscure path to the stable. Everything was silent except for servants slipping in and out of darkness with baggage. Joseph's long strides pounded the ground and his tense fingers clenched and extended as if undecided which position to take.

The stable's door was ajar. A servant, standing guard, saw Joseph and moved away. Mary and Jesus nestled in the hay like a doe and her fawn.

The dove on the manger rim dozed but opened her eyes when Joseph peeked in the door. She hopped down and scurried out the door, greeting him. She knew something was wrong, for Joseph paced. The dove flew to a nearby boulder. He saw her, went over, and sat next to her. He lowered his head, clasped his hands together, and prayed.

Joseph's chest pounded, and the muscles in his jaws twitched. Sensing his agony, the dove sat quietly with him and waited.

In a burst of frustration, Joseph sprang to his feet like a coil springing. His spirit was restless. Even though he prayed, no answers came. He needed assurance and guidance from God on how and where to flee from Herod. "Little dove, what should I do?"

The dove was distracted by a movement behind Joseph. She blinked. She could not believe what she saw. As Joseph faced her and spoke, the area behind him pulsed like a heartbeat in shimmering light. This light appeared instantly and glowed with such intensity that the iridescence spilled over Joseph and the dove. Joseph wheeled around as if expecting an attack. He staggered backward. There before him, glowing brightly, was a six-foot angel. The dove sidestepped, lost her footage on the edge of the rock, and tumbled awkwardly into the grass.

The angel's gaze followed the dove, who peeked out from the rock. The heavenly being, dressed in a simple white robe, resembled a well-built boy of eighteen years. His eyes sparkled, his brown complexion shown clear, and short auburn curls circled his head. Joseph recognized him as the angel who spoke to him in a dream a year ago concerning Mary's impending blessedness. The angel looked to Joseph. His voice was soft but commanding. "Joseph, I'm sent again from God to give you another message. Leave Bethlehem immediately and take the infant Jesus to Egypt until King Herod reigns no more. Don't be afraid. God is with you." With these words he riveted his tender gaze back to the dove. She crept from behind the rock, shifting her feet. Why was the angel looking at her?

As quickly as the angel came, he disappeared. The dove moved to the spot where the angel had stood but found nothing but shadows of the night.

Joseph held transfixed for a moment and then, recharged with new courage and direction, he called out. "We must hurry and get packed. We leave tonight for Egypt."

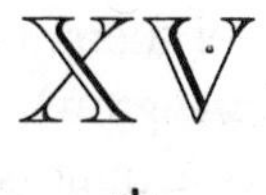

XV

❄

Joseph worked feverishly loading the donkey with baskets, gourds, and a netted bag of dried fruit. The dove and the dog planted themselves nearby like a patrol waiting for orders. Joseph tiptoed into the stable, kneeling beside sleeping Mary. He awoke her; they talked. Mary pressed her hands to her breast, let out a cry, and sobbed. Tenderly Joseph folded her in his arms, rocking her like a child.

They drew strength from each other. Then, spurred by the angel's words, they sprang into action. Mary threw on heavy winter clothing and changed Jesus, while Joseph scooped up the frankincense jar, blankets, a wash basin, and Jesus' playthings. Jesus dozed as Mary's trembling fingers swaddled him snugly in a woolen cloak. Cradling the bundle, she padded outside into the crisp night air.

The star of the east disappeared while charcoal clouds slithered over the moon's oval face. Joseph tightened the girth on the donkey. Snap! A twig broke behind him in the shadows. Alarmed, both he and Mary whirled to face the sound. Mangy dog leaped in front of them, taking a bowlegged stance, making gutteral growls. Mary pulled Jesus under her mantle as a lioness protects her cub. Joseph stared into the blackened bushes and eased Mary behind him, spying movement of a helmet and sword. Mangy dog crouched to spring when a husky voice whispered, "Hold the dog, Joseph. It's me, Maximus!"

Joseph grabbed a handful of fur, steadying the dog. Joseph edged closer to the woods. Joseph whispered, "Maximus? What are you doing here? Are you alone?"

Maximus stayed undercover, fidgeting with his sword. The whites of his eyes shone as he looked back and forth. Sweat glistened on his face and arms. The voice was breathless. "I'm alone. I'm here to warn you. Yesterday Herod called the leagues to the palace. He ordered us to Bethlehem to find the boy baby in the stable. We are to deliver the infant, along with the parents, to his majesty himself. Herod is in a bad temperament and will make an evil spectacle of the child's death. I saw it in his eyes. He's a sick man, Joseph."

Mary and Joseph inched closer to Maximus, into the bushes, out of the lantern light. Shifting his feet, Maximus continued, "I took a chance on coming, suspecting you were the couple Herod seeks. I couldn't bear to see your torture. If they capture Mary, I shudder to think what will happen to her." Joseph slipped a protective arm around Mary and Jesus. "You must leave immediately. An army of soldiers entered Bethlehem this evening. A few hours ago they set up camp, eating and drinking before the arrest.

"Don't take the main roads leading from Bethlehem. They are swarming with soldiers and spies. Being raised in this area, I know every crook and cranny. Escape through the back gate by the large cedar tree and travel the small dirt paths that wind south past the valleys and caverns. There are plenty of hiding places in the caves.

"There is an outlaw clan that lives in the caves before you get to a forsaken area called Mareshah. I was raised by these thieves. Travelers do not pass through without being stripped of everything." Maximus lowered his head, scuffling his boot on a rock. "I sent my slave boy to warn them of your coming. They will hide you. Show them my bracelet. Because I was once one of them, they will honor my wishes and protect you. You are going to need their protection. It's the only way you can escape Herod. Now go quickly. God's speed, my friends." Joseph and Maximus clasped arms firmly. Maximus turned and vanished into the night.

XVI

Joseph wheeled around facing Mary, placed both hands firmly upon her shoulders and asked, "Are you ready to run?" Bravely Mary nodded. She stared at Jesus lying motionless in her arms. Her lips moved in prayer. The dove and dog moved closer for support. Moonlight bathed the group, huddling for a brief moment, gathering courage for what lay ahead.

Caspar burst through the bushes. "Joseph, we are ready to leave. Melchior, Balthasar, and I plan to split up in three ways as a distraction to the soldiers and will meet again near Damascus. Will you go with one of us?"

Joseph clutched Mary's hand, led her to the donkey, and lifted her as he spoke. "Caspar, God is sending us in another direction. Plans are made and we are ready to leave for Egypt. We must all leave immediately. Herod's men will be here any minute."

Suddenly Balthasar and Melchior stepped onto the path, faces flushed. "We overheard. You are leaving for Egypt." The three men took a last look at the Christ Child. Tearfully they bade farewell. "Our thoughts, prayers, and love will go with you. Some day we will meet again," said Melchior. Affectionately each king grasped Mary's shaking hand and bowed before the Child.

Joseph's tense fingers checked the pouch of gold bars evenly placed around his girdle. After a quick embrace to the kings and without looking back, he tugged the donkey into a fast pace. Mangy dog loped ahead while the dove flew low. The wisemen silently slipped into the night.

The donkey's hooves clumped heavily on the cobblestones, echoing lonesomely in the dead of night. Joseph's eyes, dilated and direct, stalked the leering shadows. In the stillness he watched. He walked. He moved a comforting hand back to Mary's arm.

Thieves, beggars, drunks, prostitutes, and lepers were the usual creatures of the night. City gates shut them out at dusk, but they oozed in at the cracks. Patrolling soldiers turned blind eyes as long as they kept hidden. Decent people seldom ventured out alone. Without soldiers they were subject to attack by these pathetic creatures.

Joseph needed to get down two long streets before angling off to the back southern gate leading to the back roads. As he recalled it was the least guarded entrance. Sometimes one or two soldiers would be stationed to check pre-dawn and after dark travelers. With the census and the crowds in Bethlehem he hoped they would be tired. Joseph prayed they would be asleep, drunk, or distracted with women. Then they could slip by unnoticed.

The only ones watching as they neared the gate were a bizarre assortment of untouchables. They extended the darkness with their soiled rags, sunken eyes, and matted hair, as they strained to look at the Holy One. This underground of lowlife kept abreast of everything happening in Bethlehem, believing this child to be the promised Messiah.

The silent, staring eyes built tension in Joseph, but outwardly he remained calm and careful for Mary's sake. She sensed the tension, but looked straight ahead, anticipating a quick release from this strain.

A cock crowed as the gate banged shut behind them. Moonlight made a path into the hills. The Holy Christ Child was safely out of Bethlehem.

XVII

❄

Word spread among the untouchables that the Christ Child was safe. In pre-dawn hours, feeble hands prepared a sleeping place for the Holy Family. They pulled dried grass, stacked it in the middle of a field, and structured a sapling canopy. Eventually this rustic lean-to cradled the tired mother, father, and baby.

The builders of the night became watchers of the night. They positioned themselves as lookouts in the surrounding woods, hiding in shadows, guarding the precious family.

The untouchables had heard mystical rumors of the child's beautiful bird. Watching her, these stories seemed confirmed as she stretched her wings over the lean-to in the velvet darkness. The dove glowed like a ghost on wing, soaring, floating, and fluttering.

Like a snowdrop landing softly, she drifted down, crooning a lullaby. Succumbing to fatigue, head tucked under wing, she nestled between the child's neck and shoulder.

The dove awoke at forenoon. She flew to a branch overlooking the sleeping family. She lifted her lily throat in morning praise.

The hay rustled, arms and legs poked out, and Mary and Joseph rolled out of the grassy cocoon. Reveling in the noonday warmth, Joseph laughed and Mary pulled bits and pieces from her disheveled hair. Stomping around, they brushed themselves off.

While Mary nursed Jesus, Joseph looked around for location. Together the refugees played with and tended their son. "Where are we?" Mary asked.

"I believe we are where Maximus said we should be, near the rocky paths that lead south past the Valley of Burning."

Mary pulled a hophemp tunic over Jesus' head and laid him on a blanket on the grass. He stretched and kicked, murmuring sweetly.

Relieved after the frightening night, Mary reached for Joseph, embracing him. Alone in the middle of the field, holding hands, they knelt, bowing heads, giving thanks in morning worship.

Time was precious to their exodus. Joseph knew they needed to move on, for Herod still hunted them. Gathering Jesus, Mary mounted the donkey. The sun rose higher as Joseph led the way up the rocky footpath into the hills. The dove spiraled upward above them toward the sun. The family from Nazareth moved forward into the uncertainty ahead.

As they traveled, the runaway family ate dried fruit and drank from the waterskin, fleeing along the crooked path. Noon pressed the heat, and clouds draped the mountains like a prayer shawl.

"How are we going to get to Egypt?" Mary asked. Joseph talked over the hooves clumping on pebbles. "Once we get out of Judea, we can catch a caravan into Egypt. For now, we need to get away. Herod's soldiers are checking all main roads. Not finding us, they will start searching the back roads. We need to get as far away as possible today."

Mangy dog popped out of a thicket. His nose was layered with dirt from rooting for his breakfast. The comical vagabond, panting, took the lead. The dove circled high while the family threaded over and around boulders, bushes, and steep inclines. The skinny path led higher into the hills, shrinking Bethlehem into the valley.

Late afternoon hoofbeats pounded the trail. Mary and Joseph scurried for cover among rocks leading to a cave. Quickly Mary slid off the donkey, pulled off a large basket, swept Jesus into it, and pushed the basket inside the musty cave. The dove waddled to the basket, crouching beside it protectively. "Stay!" Joseph yelled at the dog sitting in the cave. He and Mary ran, pulling the donkey.

Down the road two soldiers halted their horses. A small boy of eight years with sandy red hair, bare feet, and sheepskin clothing stood on a boulder, towering over the men.

"Hey! Boy! Have you seen anyone traveling this road?" bellowed a husky voice.

The boy nodded, pointing a stick to the rocks hiding Mary and Joseph. "Some people are over there," he whined, nonchalantly munching an apple.

Abruptly the soldiers tight-reined their horses and began searching the pathway and cross-examining every boulder. They spied Mary and Joseph sitting on a blanket, cracking nuts.

"Ho there! In the name of King Herod, stand!" The muscular and dusty soldier drew his sword, dismounting. His stallion whinnied loudly, flinging foam from his mouth. Mary and Joseph rose slowly, sweat beading and pulses pounding. The soldier's hairy eyebrows were drawn. He poked, searched, and walked around the donkey.

Mary, steadying herself from dizziness, watched the man finger a small basket on the donkey. It contained Jesus' things. Suddenly some small raisin cakes in the next basket distracted him. He grabbed and munched them, turning to his companion, "They fit the description, but I see no infant." He wiped crumbs from his chin, putting his sword tip to Joseph's chest.

A breastplate scraped a saddlehorn. The second soldier dismounted, trudging toward the cave. "I'll check around," he said. "Maybe it's hidden."

As he approached the cave opening, a howl like a fiend starving wailed from within. The soldier froze as a high-pitched eerie whistle sounded. The hair raised on the back of the man's neck. Lately, stories in his garrison told of sorcery in these hills.

"What are you afraid of, Garth?" the first soldier shouted, marching impatiently toward the cave.

Mary gave a faint start, lifting a hand to her head. A glint off the gold bracelet flashed on the soldier's face, grabbing his attention.

Brusquely, the guard wheeled around, stepped back, and grabbed Mary's wrist. "Say... for a peasant woman you ..." he paused, mouth hanging. "Where did you get this bracelet? The insignia is familiar."

Mary concentrated on answering calmly. "A friend, Maximus, gave it to us. Maybe you know him? He is an officer."

Instantly, the soldiers dropped their threatening manner at the mention of Maximus and asked, "Are you friends of Maximus?" Mary and Joseph nodded.

"Please, we beg your pardon." The soldiers shot an uncomfortable look at each other, sheathed their swords with finality, backing away. "We are sorry to have bothered you." Without another word, the soldiers mounted their horses, straightened their helmets, and rode off. The clamor and clang of swords faded down the trail.

Mary stood motionless until the men were gone. Then quickly she lifted her skirt, ducked, and ran into the musty cave. Breathing a sigh of relief, she inspected her son playing happily with the dog and bird. "Lucky for us a little gold turned their heads. Thank You, God, for Maximus!" She hugged her baby. Joseph hugged them both. Impatient to be on their way, they hurriedly gathered and moved on.

Joseph decided to travel at night so that they would not be seen. As Mary and Joseph edged back onto the trail, the small ruffian planted himself in front of them, blocking the way. "Those soldiers were looking for you. In fact, everyone is looking for you. My family has sent me to find you. I'm sorry I told the soldiers you were there. I did not see you hide the baby." Mary stared as she looked at Joseph, who was smiling broadly. "I was wondering how we would find the people Maximus spoke of."

Jesus awoke in his mother's arms. He looked around for his pet dove. The dove flew from Joseph to Mary's arm. Jesus babbled and the dove cooed.

The small stranger froze, as if hypnotized. His dark olive eyes riveted upon the child and the dove. In a whisper, almost reverently, forgetting his errand, the boy moved forward in slow motion. He inched toward this apparition, half speaking to himself saying, "Everyone is arguing and taking sides at our camp. Some say the child Herod seeks is a special king. Others don't care, siding with the soldiers in hopes of claiming a reward. I didn't believe a baby could be a king. The babies in our camp drive me crazy with crying and wet pants. I also heard rumors about a white bird, but I didn't believe that either. But now . . ." The boy stopped at the feet of Mary, looking up at

Jesus. Mesmerized by the picture, he stared at Jesus' ringlets of golden curls shimmering in the sunlight, haloing his happy face. To the boy, a glow of unexplained magic circled both the baby and His bird.

"How did they get to be friends? What does the bird say when it talks to the baby?" the boy whispered to Mary. "I'm not sure," answered Mary, "but whatever it is, you can see it is very special. There are ways of talking where words aren't needed."

Wistfully the boy responded, "I wish I had a magical bird to talk with me."

Mary lifted the dove, handing it to the boy. The boy's face lit like a thousand rainbows. His fingers slipped under the warm, crouching breast, feet gripping securely. He stood enchanted, cradling the velveteen jewel.

Walking in circles, the dove bobbing on his finger, the boy talked and talked. "Hi! I'm Benaiah. I live in the cave camps near here. I think you are beautiful. Would you like to come and see where I live?" The dove answered with tilted head and responding coos.

Joseph grabbed Mary's hand, tugging the donkey forward. He called over his shoulder. "We need to keep moving. Talk to the bird while you show us the way."

Twilight sprinkled her last rays of light before Benaiah and the small procession reached the caves.

Salina sat cross-legged in a hammock patching a tear in her husband's shirt. Restlessly she shifted her aching legs as the last ray of sunshine disappeared from the mouth of the cave dwelling.

Cam, her five-year-old daughter, blind since birth, squatted, rocking sideways in a corner. The sucking on her fingers reminded Salina of the only sound she ever made. Today the frail child annoyed her.

Wearily, she pulled herself up, slipping her swollen feet into broken sandals. Flopping across the dirt floor to the fireplace, the cold rock walls closed in on her. With heaviness inside, she peeled carrots for supper.

Salina heaved a deep sigh as sounds of her children's bickering reached her. She thought, "How in God's name, after being raised in a good Jewish home, have I allowed my family to be raised heathens in a community of thieves? I have been blind all these years to think my life would get better. It has become worse." Feeling sorry for herself, the dam broke, releasing pent-up tears.

Shortly Rickah bounded barefoot through the archway. Wiping her eyes with her apron, Salina forced a smile. "Rickah, would you please take Cam for a walk?"

"Sure, Mama." The slender body, ripe as a golden peach, reached for her sister. Cam grabbed Rickah's auburn curls tumbling around her, rubbbing them against her cheek. With bundle in arms, tousling, kissing, laughing, Rickah disappeared out the door.

Salina loved all her children — Rickah, Tynon, Benaiah and Cam. Of the four, Rickah was the least demanding. Most daughters were married by fourteen years, but Rickah, with a mind of her own, convinced her father, Giacomo, to wait before finding a suitable match for her. Usually suitors were picked from the community, but Rickah would have nothing to do with the rogues.

Salina pulled her black hair back, tying it with a leather strand, the tail reaching to her waist. Her thoughts were interrupted when her husband stomped through the entrance. The long-limbed man, arms tattooed, carried bows and arrows. He stormed to the brewing pot. "Isn't dinner ready yet? I'm starving!" Dipping his forefinger into a bowl with a cabbage mixture, he slurped what he could get into his mouth, juice sliding into his red beard. "There's fresh quail outside, woman. Get a move on you! Clean them before they swell!"

Salina sighed, shuffled outside into the dark, and picked up the birds. Loud jangling disturbed the woods. The men's traps!

The snares, strung with bells, threaded the sunken pathways. The noise in the night alerted the community of robbers that unfortunate travelers passed through their territory.

The woods burst with activity. Flaring torches lit scruffy faces. Men ran helter skelter, weapons in hand. The leader, Giacomo, wheeled a spiked club shouting, "Aha! The traps are hit! Booty tonight!" The dozen men knew their attack well. Giving quick hand signals, Giacomo directed the robbers as they swooped to the woods like vultures.

Shortly before, Mary and Joseph and Benaiah stumbled along a dismal trail. "Benaiah, it's getting too dark and there's no moon or stars to light the way. Do you think it's wise we push on?" inquired Joseph anxiously.

Just as Benaiah started to reply, Joseph and the donkey found feet and fetlocks stumbling in cords, bells attached. Ringing broke the silence of the woods. The boy stopped short. Clenching his fists, he shouted. "Oh, no, I forgot about the traps!"

Twelve fiercesome men with wicked intentions closed slowly around the family. Torch flames licked eagerly like hungry snakes. Looking up, Mary gasped. The donkey bolted sideways, startling Jesus.

Suddenly the mangy dog, fangs bared, sprang from the shadows. He was too slow. Giacomo's club pounded his ribs, crumpling him in a heap, red trickling from his side. Hideously he yelped, flopping, then crumpling.

Disbelief on his face, Joseph reached for the dog, touching the blood. Mary burst into tears. The vagabond tried lifting his faithful head. Blackness moved in. He fell limp.

Benaiah shouted, "Stop! These are my friends!"

A sword tip pricked Joseph's chest, its pressure backing him away from the dog. The man, Tank, ignored Benaiah and held Joseph's eyes. His stomach rose and fell in heavy rhythm. Groping backwards, Joseph found Mary's quivering fingers.

Weasel, grinning with yellowed teeth, shoved next to Giacomo, slapping him on the back. "Now ain't that some young beauty on the donkey?"

The thieves waited, salivating, for Giacomo's signal to tear into the couple, to ransack their belongings and have the woman. The contest challenged everyone's grabbing abilities. With sporting rules, children and infants were removed first before the fighting. In the end, the spoils were returned to a storage cave for community use, and the women were raped and turned loose in the woods, the men beaten and left on the main highway.

Giacomo's eyes narrowed, eyeing the baby. "Is that a boy?" he growled. Mary looked at Joseph, bit her quivering lip, and nodded.

Giacomo, chin hard and ruthless, motioned for Tank to take the baby from the mother. Jesus, awake, stared wide-eyed at the tormentors. Tank stepped forward. Mary's body stiffened, tightening her grip on Jesus. Suddenly, Tank stopped. Something deep within held him back. Stupored, he gawked at Giacomo, mumbling, "I can't take this baby from its mother. I don't know why, but I can't." Tank dropped his head, shifting his feet. The men roared with laughter.

Giacomo gritted his teeth, hissing. "Weasel! Get that baby!" Weasel bounced Tank out of the way and went for the baby. The baby's eyes stunned Weasel. He too was stupified. Turning slowly around, he stammered, "I can't do it either,

Gio." The men slapped their thighs, guffawing with amusement.

In a rage Giacomo pounced forward, grabbed Weasel and Tank, each hand flinging them backwards. He lunged. Powerful hands landed, tearing the child from Mary. Mary screamed. Joseph steadied her. For a few seconds not a movement was made, nor a breath was taken, as Giacomo dropped his raging eyes, looking into the face of Jesus.

The men, still having fun at Giacomo's expense, became rowdy. Giacomo, still in command, not letting his eyes leave the child, motioned his men to silence. Looking into the eyes of the child, something squeezed Giocomo's heart. In one second he understood his wretchedness, taking him into a place of all knowing. He too stood dumbfounded. Suddenly, the thieves realized something profound had taken them over.

Suspecting witchcraft, the uneasy men fidgeted and mumbled among themselves.

At this moment a bent figure crept into the lantern's circle of light. The old woman was Merna, the midwife. She was the community doctor, prophetess, and spiritual leader. She knew all, her ears and mind sharp as a butcher's knife.

Lifting a bony finger, her high-pitched voice croaked a warning. Shuffling back and forth, she spoke, hands moving like a gypsy reading a crystal ball.

My men, beware of a fearful night,
When strangers come into your sight.
A Child of gold will pierce you through,
To change your soul and start anew.
He carries with Him a bird of white,
The Ghost of God on winged flight,
Herod seeks this holy one,
He plans to kill the firstborn sons.

Heed this warning everyone.
Do not let his plan be done!

Merna's voice stabbed the night. Everyone stood transfixed. The soothsayer's wisdom was respected. Merna rubbed her stubbled chin, racing her cat-like eyes over the men. Hobbling over to Mary, she intently looked into Mary's eyes. Gently picking up the trembling arm, she slid back the sleeve, exposing the circlet. Moving to Giacomo, she whispered in his ear. Unruly white hair flapped in her face as she turned, slinking back into the shadows.

Just then Benaiah breathlessly shouted again, "These people can't be taken. They are friends of Maximus!" As Benaiah came into the circle of light, the dove, who had been riding on his shoulder, spotted Jesus, and sprang upward. She fluttered around the heads of the thieves, landing on Jesus' shoulder. Her whiteness reflected a glow in the night, giving a shining appearance in the darkness.

Weasel stepped backward, pointing. "It's God's white ghost!" The men backed slowly away. Fearlessly Benaiah strode to his father's side. Giacomo snapped out of his trance. He peered sharply into the darkness where Merna had disappeared. Still holding the baby, he gruffly shouted, "My son is right! These people are friends of Maximus." Surprise engulfed the men.

Rumbling of voices rose. "Silence!" Giacomo commanded. "Maximus sends word that we are to protect them at all cost."

Giacomo lifted Jesus over his head, bellowing, "Herod plans to slaughter this boy! He is propheted to be our leader some day." Giacomo brought the child down, continuing. "The mother and father will not be touched. They will stay in my cave until an escape is made." Eyes lowered, Giacomo carefully handed Jesus to Mary, then turned, glaring fiercely at his men. "If any man here challenges my order, let him do so now!" The leader's upper lip lifted slightly. Weasel and Tank slowly side-stepped next to him. Exchanging glances, the gang of thieves hesitated, slackening grips on their weapons.

Giacomo picked up his club, signaling his men to disperse for the night. Reluctantly they drifted away. Low grumbles echoed in the woods. Weasel and Tank stayed.

Rushing to the dog, Benaiah shouted, "What can we do for the dog?" Giacomo shifted his feet, looking down. Tank spoke up. "Forget him. He's a goner. Let's go. We're hungry!"

Giacomo found his voice. "Ben, show this couple and their son to our cave. Take care of their donkey." Gathering to leave, he paused deep in thought, and looked down at the weapon in his hands. "If the dog is still alive, you can take care of him. See if Merna can help."

He left, Weasel and Tank following.

Mary kneeled beside the dog,with Jesus balanced on her hip. She leaned over the dog and stroked his head. Soft whimpers wafted from deep within the dog's chest. Joseph approached with swathing bands. "We can't really tell how bad he is but he is still breathing. Let's wrap his ribcage securely."

Benaiah helped Joseph bandage the dog's ribs. Joseph fashioned a small stretcher from saplings and a blanket. Carefully they lifted the dog onto it. Benaiah stood up, asking, "May the dog sleep with me tonight? The dove and I will talk to him so he will want to live. I can get Merna early in the morning. Please?" Joseph nodded a concerned approval.

The dove hopped onto the edge of the stretcher, and together the group carried the suffering dog to Giacomo's cave.

XX

The wind whistled through the cracks of the cave as Salina stirred the carrot soup. Restlessly she waited to hear news of the visitors, and the booty of the traps, not expecting that they would both come at once. Giacomo slipped into the doorway, slowly dropped his club against the wall, trudged to a stool, and sat down. He leaned forward, clasping his hands to his face. Salina, wiping hands on her apron, turned to him. "Well?"

For the first time in their twenty-year marriage, the big man looked pleadingly to his wife. Something appeared in his eyes she had never seen before. It was compassion mixed with sorrow. A spark, flickering deep within, drew her to his side.

He spoke faintly, humbly. "Salina, years ago I fought in Samaria, capturing you, a twelve-year-old girl. I dragged you here, making you my wife. You were a frightened kitten. You remember?" Salina nodded.

Haltingly, he reached for her hand. Salina's heart pounded. "The first years you withdrew from me, spending hours in prayer. This infuriated me, and challenged me to break you. I ridiculed and mimicked you in front of the men. I remember being in a drunken stupor and dragging you to our campfires, forcing you to recite your beliefs, and mocking your answers with revelry. My men loved the show, and it made me feel powerful."

Giacomo sat silent for a moment, took a deep breath, and gave Salina an embarrassed glance. "Do you also remember what you said about a Holy Child to be born in Bethlehem who would be a Mighty Counselor, an Everlasting King, a Messiah?" Giacomo mumbled, "I ridiculed you, but now, I'm sorry." Covering his face with his hands, he wept.

Salina was awestruck. This wasn't the same man she knew an hour before. "Gio," she said softly, "what has happened?"

Giacomo lifted his head, staring at his hands. "Tonight I met this Holy Child. I was so blinded by greed and power, I almost didn't see Him. When I grabbed Him from his mother, I don't know what happened to me. It was a strange feeling. Looking into the Child's eyes, I knew without hesitation that something profound had changed me. I also knew I was holding the Messiah. I just knew! Salina, how could that be? How could I know something as certain just like that?" Salina anwered, "It's God's way. Trust Him."

Giacomo jumped up, pacing. "I knew we were having guests that Maximus wanted us to protect. But now I know I have invited the Holy Family to stay in our home. We must help them escape because Herod is looking for them. I may have difficulty because some of the men reacted to my command strangely. Herod is offering a reward for anyone turning the baby in."

Towering over Salina, Giacomo placed his hands upon her shoulders. "My life as a thief has not been right, but I've known no other way." Excitedly he shouted, "This baby, this King, accepted me! Me! Giacomo, the great captain of thieves!" He took her hands, biting his lip. "Will you help me protect this Child? If I do one thing right in my life — this will be it."

Salina didn't have to answer. Beaming a smile such as he had never seen before, she threw her arms around her husband, kissing him.

Together, they waited for the Christ Child to enter their home.

XXI

Shyly, Mary and Joseph entered Giacomo's cave. Salina's heart jumped as she pressed Jesus to her breast, cradling Him. How long she had waited! The children gathered around, while Giacomo carried Cam over to touch the baby. Jesus babbled sounds, making the little girl clap her hands and laugh. The dove and mangy dog added to the commotion of the moment.

The two families gathered for supper, the Holy Family in exile and the thievish family in turmoil. Sitting on low stools around a mahogany table, they shared carrot soup, warm bread with honey, date pudding, and wine. At first Giacomo was ill at ease with Mary and Joseph. He was quiet and kept his eyes lowered. The tension broke as Salina and Benaiah told stories. Everyone laughed when Benaiah encouraged the dove to eat date pudding from the top of his head.

Like a stone, the mangy dog lay on his stretcher. Benaiah checked continually on his condition. Stubbornly, Cam positioned herself next to the animal, his warmth comforting her. Benaiah guided her hand to the dog's head, showing her how to stroke. He said, "This will help the doggie get better." Rocking sideways, making sucking noises, she petted his head.

After dinner Salina showed Mary and Joseph the toilette in an adjoining alcove. Inside were a water basin and towels upon a wooden table. Nearby, on a short ledge, a small opening in the rocks dropped ten feet or more to an underground stream. Joseph was impressed with the practicality of cave life.

Bedding for the night in the main cave, Mary and Joseph arranged their blankets in a hammock strung from pegs wedged between rocks.

Late into the night Mary and Joseph curled in the wide hammock, Jesus sleeping between them. Holding Mary in his arms, Joseph recited the prayers of his forefathers, giving thanks to God. The dove's croon, echoing in the dark, lulled everyone to sleep.

In the early morning hours Benaiah, sprawled in his swinging bed, suddenly remembered the dog.

He bounded out of bed, threw on his sheepskin vest, and raced out the door.

Bumping a table, Benaiah woke everyone. Giacomo had already gone, and had left empty sheaths for hunting equipment on a bench. Salina arose, poked the embers in the fireplace, and added kindling. A teakettle rattled; she filled it with water and hung it over a wobbling flame. The spicy smells of tea leaves sprinkled in the water filled the room. Mary and Joseph arose, dressed, and helped with breakfast.

Soon Merna entered the cave, with Benaiah holding her hand. She nodded solemnly to each person. Joseph swung Jesus in the hammock. Nearing the infant, Merna stopped, clasped both hands as in supplication, and stooped over the Child. Mumbling to herself, she made a sign in the air. Tugging her sleeve, Benaiah pulled her away. Merna grinned toothlessly, patted Joseph's shoulder, and turned to the dog.

The woman's bones clicked as she lowered herself to the floor. Carefully she probed and examined. The dove stood near following every movement. She turned to the boy saying, "He might make it. If he wakens, give him water and soft food. Don't move him." Benaiah nodded.

Hugging the boy, she murmured, "The will to live is the greatest medicine in the world."

The dove stepped in front of them. "Ah! So this is the magical bird of the Child." She stroked the silky throat and whispered, "Yes, it shall come to pass."

Just then Giacomo entered the cave swinging the catch of the day. "Hah!" he roared. "Quail and rabbit for a feast tonight in honor of our guests." The lifeless forms landed, thumping a cutting board. Suddenly Cam jerked her head from sleep, groping until she felt the dog. She shouted, "My dog! My dog!" Feeling Merna's arm, she pushed the woman's arm away. Hugging the dog, she continued stroking him. "My dog!"

Salina dropped a handful of spoons, grabbing Giacomo. "Her first words!" she cried. Salina, Giacomo, Tynon, Rickah and Benaiah ran to Cam, surrounding her. Hugging each other, they shouted and patted the dog with her. "Your dog! Yes, Cam! Your dog!"

Excited, Benaiah took the dove and danced around the room. Merna started for the door, then stopped, looking troubled. "The wind carries the wailing of anguished mothers. Herod knows the child-king has escaped. In fury he is slaying all the firstborn babies under two years. Every road is blocked."

Joseph's jaws tightened with this news. He looked at Mary who was turning pale. Merna paused, eyed Jesus in Mary's arms, and said, "If you are wise, you will get Giacomo to move you out immediately. The escape map that leads to the western caravan trails is kept by the Elders of the Council. This route hasn't been used for years, but you would be wise to use it." Merna's eyes searched each face. "God be with you, my children." The old woman shook her head, turned, and hobbled out of the cave.

Everyone was silent. Thoughts jumbled their minds — the joy with Cam, mangy dog, and the massacres in Bethlehem.

Later that morning rain pelted against the rock walls. Everyone busied himself inside the cave. Salina worked with Cam practicing new words, hope soaring with each new sentence. Cam's hand continued to stroke the dog.

Benaiah and Tynon played a game of knucklebone. The playing pieces carved from sandstone bounced against the rocky wall. Benaiah hollered, "Gotchya, Tynon!"

"Lower your voice, Benaiah," Salina remonstrated. Giacomo and Joseph sat at a table studying a yellowed map. "Tomorrow Tynon and I will lead you through this rocky passage. It will be difficult climbing, but it's the only way to get out safely."

In a corner of the room, a basin of water next to her, Mary bathed Jesus while sitting on a low stool. The Child kicked freely in a towel on her lap. She sponged his chubby legs. Intense thoughts of the baby massacres and their safety made her little aware of what was going on around her. Her concentration broke when Rickah pulled a stool beside her.

Mary smiled at the girl. The same age as herself, Rickah admired the young mother.

"Mary, are you afraid?" Rickah asked, putting a finger in the Child's hand. He grasped it tightly, breaking into a gurgle.

"No, Rickah. I know God will watch over His Son. God is with me and He makes the way easy to endure."

Rickah reached for the basin of water, setting it on her lap so it would be closer to Mary. "I wish I had your faith."

Mary smiled softly. "It's not hard to find. Just as God planted the seed of this little boy in me, He can plant the seed of faith in you."

Mary glanced over at Joseph, laid a hand on Rickah's arm and whispered, "Being brave is easier when you have a loving husband who stands by your side."

Rickah fingered her skirt and leaned closer to her friend. "Mary, Joseph is much older than you, isn't he?"

"Yes, I grew up admiring him. There has never been anyone for me except Joseph. He says he has always loved me, too."

"Were your parents upset with you when you wanted to marry him?"

Mary lifted Jesus, rolling Him to His stomach on her lap. "At first, very much. I had other pursuers my mother fancied, but Joseph was patient and won my parents' trust. They finally let Joseph and me become betrothed. My parents also changed as our lives became entwined with God. Because of Joseph's total support for me in my difficult condition, my parents grew to love him."

Mary felt a stab of homesickness. She was escaping to Egypt with Jesus and her family had not yet seen her baby.

Rickah grabbed Mary's shoulder. "Oh, Mary, this is so exciting! Can I talk to you about my problem?" She lowered her voice, looking around to see if anyone was listening. She blurted her secret.

"Maximus and I love each other!"

Mary stopped washing Jesus' hand, and looked directly at Rickah. Rickah's eyes danced as she spoke. "Nineteen years ago he was stolen. Merna gave him to my mother, thinking an infant would help her in the childless marriage.

"Mother adored Maximus. When he was seven years old, I was born. Then came Tynon, Ben, and Cam. I grew up following Maximus everywhere. I adored him and he cared for me like a brother. When a boy of this community reaches eighteen years of age, he has the option to leave the clan. If he makes the decision to leave, he takes a vow never to return or make mention of our way of life to anyone in the outside world. Most men choose to stay, take wives, and become members of the notorious group.

"But Maximus was different. Even though he was the bravest and most fierce of fighters, he didn't feel comfortable with the thievish way of life. He was one of the few who chose to leave the community. Although it broke my parents' heart to see him leave, my mother later confided in me that she admired him.

"The night before Maximus left, we met in the olive grove to say goodbye. I was twelve years old. We realized our love was more than brother and sister love. We vowed our grown-up love for each other. Maximus said as soon as he established himself in the outside world, he would come back for me."

Rickah twisted her fingers; concern contorted her mouth. "Mary, I've waited two years and I can't hold my parents much longer on my betrothal. I've convinced my father no suitor pleases me. I've stalled telling Father until I heard from Maximus. Last summer a letter came along with a bracelet. He said he had a top-paying job as a Roman officer. As soon as he received a new station, he'd plead my case with my parents. Lately my father has been very short with me concerning my betrothal. Do you think I am being silly to hope and wait?"

Mary remembered Maximus' hazel eyes, his powerful build, jovial manner, and kind soul.

"No, Rickah, you are a fool if you don't fight for him. We found Maximus a fine and caring person. If it weren't for him, we wouldn't be here, away from Herod."

Mary fingered the gold bracelet. Rickah smiled, laid back her tunic on her arm, revealing an identical bracelet. The girls laughed. They knew Roman soldiers often brutally struck out at innocent people. A simple tag system with an identifying bracelet, necklace, pin, hairpiece, or earring kept soldiers of the same garrison from harming each other's friends or relatives.

Mary leaned over and hugged Rickah. "I'm glad you love Maximus and I hope your marriage comes true. Great love is a gift that only comes to a few. If you and Maximus have a chance to be blessed as Joseph and I, by all means, wait for him. Hold fast to your dream and do not waver. Don't give in to anything less. It is worth the wait. If you strongly believe, wonderful love will happen."

Rickah threw her arms around her friend. "Oh, Mary! Thank you!"

Mary, beaming, finished tying a string overlapping Jesus' shirt. Lifting him, kissing him on the nose, she handed him to Rickah. The Infant clasped her sweetly around the neck. He smelled like fresh lilacs. Warm feelings of pure joy encircled the young woman.

An infectious giggle exploded from Cam's corner. Everyone turned to see mangy dog, head slightly raised, weakly licking Cam under her chin. "My doggie. He loves me," she cried. The frail arms hugged the shaggy head.

Tynon, with a gangling stride, raced over to Cam, crouching down. "Wow, a whole string of words. That's great, Cammy!" He tousled the red hair, her blind eyes following his voice.

Salina and Benaiah raced for the food pail, joined Cam, and carefully placed soft tidbits of biscuits dipped in gravy into the dog's mouth. Chewing slowly, he gulped unrefined, obviously in pain. Nevertheless he enjoyed the attention. His tail flopped feebly like a palsied hand.

Giacomo walked over, watching, swallowing hard. Having never felt love in his home before, he watched it perform miracles. A new direction for life was seeding itself in this man.

Later that day Joseph and Mary removed the bandages from the mangy dog, carefully cleansing the gashes in the ribcage. Ragged blanket tucked under her arm, Cam bent over the dog, talking into his ear. Cam's need to express herself, after all the silent years, poured out in practice sentences. Naming the dog Argus, after a giant in a story

Rickah had told her of a giant with a hundred eyes, Cam declared, "You, Argus. You be Cam's eyes!" Other pairs of eyes seeing this scene were instantly damp.

Lightning cracked, splitting the sky, followed by a peal of thunder. Mary and Joseph met each other's concerned looks. How could they leave in this storm?

Alone, Maximus lay upon a cot in an officer's quarter. He tossed, sat up, and turned sideways on the bed, running his hands through thick hair. Clasping his hands together he set his elbows on his knees, remaining there with chin resting upon white knuckles. The young man stared intently out the window. He leaned back, arms behind his head, and stared at the sun breaking through the clouds. "I wish I could forget what is going on with my men in the courtyard," he thought. "How glad I am that I took a three-day absence, but I am devastated about the blood of children. The massacres are far worse than anything I grew up with in the clan."

Maximus leaned forward and clasped his brown palms around the sill, digging his nails into the wood. "I am ashamed for Rome. I cannot stay in Judea and serve under Herod's tyranny. It is tearing me apart." Maximus stood and paced. "My requested change in duty will not come soon enough. The choice either to be promoted to high rank here or serve as a commander in a remote territory of Decapolis was not a hard one to make. I believe I can be a just and sensible ruler in this northern village. I want Rickah to start this new life with me as my wife, but I'm afraid Giacomo and Salina would never break clan rules to let her go that far. Even then I'm not sure if Rickah still loves me." The soldier sat very still as he contemplated, then quickly decided to send his proposal message to Rickah immediately.

When the messengers arrived at the cave, the two families were clearing dishes after a large dinner of quail and rabbit. A hubbub of noise! Everyone crowded around. Rickah was the first to understand the significance of the letter. She untied it and read it. Rickah glanced at Mary with a hidden smile, then drew her parents aside for a talk.

Cam sat loyally by her dog's side. Since the storm had subsided, Mary and Joseph finished packing the donkey outside the cave and spent time rebandaging the mangy dog. Leaving Rickah,

Salina, and Giacomo still talking, they quietly went off to bed. Before dawn they would leave to escape to Egypt.

In the dead of night, outside Giacomo's cave, men's voices spoke low. A torch flickered as Maximus talked with Tank and Weasel. Maximus held his helmet under his arm and fingered the sword at his waist.

"Someone from the clan, hungering for the reward, reported the peasant couple and the Holy Child staying in Giacomo's cave. Herod is sending a regiment of three hundred soldiers, along with fifteen choice gladiators. They are camping five miles north of here and will have this place smudged out by noon tomorrow."

Nervously Tank shifted, as Weasel spit on the ground growling, "Let them come. We are a fighting match for any Roman rogues!" Maximus raised a hand to Weasel's shoulder. "We'll warn the women, children, and elders. If the fighters want to stay, that's their choice. I want to get Mary, Joseph, and Jesus an early lead into the escape route."

"Giacomo plans to take them out early tomorrow morning," Weasel responded.

"Good, then they will be already packed," Maximus said. "I want Rickah to leave with me. After Herod announced his attack plans, I came quickly on the back roads with a cart to get Rickah's family out. Herod has given me orders to leave for my new command post, so moving up north with them would be safe. Wait until we all leave and then give us one hour before alerting the rest of the clan. You men are welcome to catch up with us later."

Tank and Weasel shook their heads. "No, we'll stay and fight. We have always waited for the big one."

"Thank you... and good luck," Maximus said. He slammed both men squarely on the shoulders with his fists as he had many times when growing up. Weasel and Tank gave toothless grins, heading back to their posts.

Maximus sneaked cautiously into the dark cave, found Giacomo's hammock, and carefully nudged him awake. There was an exchange of identification, the sound of a firm armclasp, followed by a long conversation of whispers. Soon Giacomo sprang up, fumbling with a candle. Once lit, the big man bellowed like a walrus, "Wake up!"

Everyone looked up dazed, lifting squinting eyes from under blankets. Giacomo announced Maximus' arrival and explained their danger.

"Tynon and I will leave immediately with Mary, Joseph, and Jesus as planned. Salina, Rickah, Benaiah, and Cam! Dress quickly and leave with Maximus. Tynon and I will eventually join you in the northern village that will be our new home. By the way, I guess this is Rickah's betrothal announcement to Maximus." Giacomo looked at Salina, with hand over her mouth, and watering eyes, then shifted his gaze to Rickah as she sprang out of bed. "You both have our blessings." There was a pause, then he growled, "Tynon, load the dog in the cart for Cam. Now! Everyone, move fast!"

Rickah bounded to Maximus, who had been watching her closely. Even in her cotton nightgown and tousled hair she looked radiant as she threw her arms around his neck, crying, "I knew you would come!"

Maximus lowered his voice. "I thought I was going to have a major battle on my hands with your father. I can't believe he went along with my plan. What's happened here?"

Rickah kissed him on the cheek. "The Child made the difference. I'll tell you all about it later. Let's get going."

The families raced about in the dark, everyone talking at once. Mary and Joseph, having packed the night before, blanketed Jesus and moved outside with the others. Maximus loaded the dog and food into the small horse-drawn cart.

Mary took Jesus to the wagon to say goodbye to the mangy dog. Jesus reached small fingers forward, touching the dog's head. The dove joined to say goodbye. With Joseph's hand upon her shoulder, Mary whispered, stroking the dog, "Goodbye, Argus. We love you. We know you are going to get well. Take good care of Cam."

Eyes were teary as everyone hugged and said farewell in the starlit night. Mary promised Rickah that some day, when she returned to Galilee, she would visit her.

Benaiah had one last talk with the dove. Salina kissed her husband. Joseph slipped Maximus a gold bar as a wedding gift and once again thanked his friend for his help.

With the donkey loaded, Giacomo, Tynon, Mary, Joseph, Jesus, and the dove fled quickly through a narrow rock passage leading south to the desert. With the cart loaded, Maximus, Rickah, Salina, Benaiah, Cam, and Argus headed north to begin a new life.

❄

Fortunately, the stars and moon lit the way for the Holy Family. Traveling slowly, Giacomo and Tynon led them single file through difficult terrain. Nature held her breath in the moonlight at the passing of the Holy One. An owl hooted greetings from an old yew tree. A lizard paused under a mustard bush, and a silver fox sat silent with her cubs watching from the mouth of her den.

Hours passed, and the only sound echoing was the clop-clopping of the donkey's hooves upon the gravel path. Giacomo announced they would rest near a cave called Echidna's Den.

Dawn broke as the group rested at the mouth of the cave. They passed around a waterskin and nibbled dried figs. A ram's horn trumpeted far off. Giacomo traced a triangle with his finger in the dust. Sweat glistening on his red mustache, he squinted a concerned look at Tynon. "That was the Roman attack signal. The clan families should be well on their way to this cove. They are about an hour behind us. Let's hope the remaining men had enough sense to flee. We are no match for gladiators."

Tynon looked earnestly at his father. "Weasel will do a great job at holding them. It's in his blood — anyway, if they do survive, he is cream for leadership." Tynon paused, then put a hand on Giacomo's shoulder. "Dad? I'm glad we're together." Giacomo fidgeted and Tynon slapped his hand out, clasping his dad's arm in the warrior fashion. "I can't wait to get to the new village. Maximus told me I would make a fine soldier in his garrison." Giacomo swallowed hard and pressed an assuring hand to his son's shoulder.

Giacomo cautiously led them into Echidna's Den. The great room's walls displayed primitive writing, pictures of exiles, and refugees of the past. Mary stared at a drawing of a peasant girl weeping. Her black hair tumbled around her. She kneeled at a grave. Where her tears fell, lilies of glorious colors sprouted. Mary, noticing, felt a lump rise in her throat.

The small caravan wound its way slowly to the back of the cave, where they hunted for two obelisk-like rocks marking the spot into a tunnel. This was the final part of the escape route, one that was rarely used. No one had entered the tunnel for many years. Giacomo did not know where it led or where it came out. He knew only what the clan's map showed: it would come out on the southwest end of the rocky hills and meet with a caravan route to the west.

Giacomo unpacked two torches from the donkey, lit them, and gave one to Tynon. Gravely looking at Mary and Joseph, he said, "We will enter single file with the donkey. Tynon will bring up the rear. Keep close and do not make any loud noises in case of bats, loose rocks, and sifting dirt."

Joseph gave Jesus to Mary, taking a firm hold on the donkey. Mary drew her mantle over the baby's face and hunched her shoulders protectively. One by one they entered the black hole in the cave.

The tunnel closed around them as they felt their way deeper into the gaping mouth of the rock. They heard nothing and saw nothing but moved forward, the flickering torch lighting only a few feet at a time.

Mary felt coldness, the air thickening and smelling musty. Pushing thoughts of lizards and snakes out of her mind, she concentrated on protecting her baby.

The dove, sensitive to confinement, gripped Joseph's shoulder. His muscles were tense.

Giacomo's heart pounded with a fear of the unknown in the living tomb of blackness. His driving need to save the Child kept him from returning. There was no turning back.

Suddenly Giacomo splashed into icy cold water; it pulled him up sharp and short. He didn't know whether it was a deep pool or the lip of an underground stream crossing the floor of the tunnel. He picked up a pebble, tossing it forward. Plunk! It hit stone.

"Good!" Giacomo whispered over his shoulder. "It's only a thin stream. I think we can wade through. Let me go first to see how deep or slippery it might be."

The stream proved to be only ankle deep. Joseph hoisted Mary and Jesus on the donkey, wading into the icy water. Tynon followed but the air was so thin that his torch's flame weaved like a drunken yeoman.

Over the stream and up an incline they stopped, regrouping to knit closer. Unexpectedly both torches shriveled, extinguishing. Total blackness!

There were a few silent moments of disbelief until Tynon groped forward, feeling his father, who stiffened. Joseph pulled Mary and Jesus into his arms, holding them protectively. The donkey blew his nostrils, the only one unconcerned.

Clearing his throat, Giacomo muttered, "We are lost. It's almost impossible to start torches with bad air."

From the depth of blackness came the unison of Mary and Joseph's voices, words piercing the abyss of fear.

> The Lord is my light and my salvation;
> Whom shall I fear?
> The Lord is the strength of my life;
> Of whom shall I be afraid?
>
> (Psalm 27:1)

After the words, everyone stood silently in the blackness, eyes adjusting. The only sound was water dripping. They waited. In a few minutes, Tynon yelled, "Look ahead!" A tiny pinhole of light could barely be seen in the distance. Groping carefully, they inched forward like blind children learning to walk. The pinhole of light opened wider until the group burst into the glorious warmth of sunlight.

Like butterflies emerging cocoons, they fluttered about rejoicing. Tynon did a cartwheel in the green grass. Giacomo threw his arms around Mary, Joseph, and Jesus in a giant bear hug. The dove took flight, soaring like an eagle higher and higher. She fluttered, flipped, and floated downward toward the laughing Child, and then struck skyward as if carrying the thankful prayers heavenward.

Looking out over the flat horizon, the group could see the colored sand of the desert. Giacomo knew they were near the southern border of Judea, a non-populated area.

Within a few miles was a shelter and water station for camel caravans heading into Egypt. By noon they arrived at the small post where they relaxed in an adobe shelter, eating lunch. The sun scorched them by afternoon but they cooled off in a watering hole nearby.

Heralding a cool evening wind, a caravan of sixty Bedouin tribesmen and their families soon appeared. Joseph negotiated a payment in gold bars in return for protection into Egypt. The agreement was sealed with a handshake.

Giacomo and Tynon waved farewell to Mary, Joseph, Jesus, and the dove as they melted into the line with camels. Against a vermilion sunset, they stood and watched the long caravan shrink into the desert sand.

XXV

Due to the cooling winds, refreshing after the blistering sun, the caravan moved into the night. The endless line strung in the moonlight, shadows high upon the backs of camels, rocking rhythmically onward like ships over the waves. Swaying lanterns beaconed in the night.

Chilling winds set in, shifting hills of treacherous sand. Mary, her face wrapped in tangled mantel, felt small on the donkey, shadowed by the monstrous camels. Joseph, head bent against the desert's lash, tugged on the donkey. Jesus and the dove lay in a basket, covered with protective cloth, strapped to the donkey's side.

They slept their first night on the desert with wind whistling and sand piling. They felt the heat as the sun peeked over the horizon. Digging their way out of the mounds of brown sugar, they stretched their cramped legs. Knowing they wouldn't travel with the intense heat, Joseph and Mary set up camp with a temporary lean-to made of blankets, protecting them from the burning rays.

A plump woman, covered with a black woolen overgarment with only her face showing, trudged over with a milk jug. "Water is precious on the desert, and we must use it sparingly, but we have plenty of camel milk and you may help yourself to all you need from the camel driver. Since there is little water, we wash our babies and ourselves with camel urine. That you can also get from the camel driver. I am Hajaja and if you need anything or have any questions, just ask for me." Abruptly she plopped the jug in the sand, camel milk dripping down the sides, and waddled away.

"Well, Mary," said Joseph, winking and giving Mary a squeeze, "I can't wait to find out what else we need to know." Mary, hands on hips, staring after the woman, rolled her eyes, saying, "My grandmother showed me how to clean everything with the water from desert plants. Let's hope we can find them. I'll show you what to look for." She looked skyward, as if speaking to the heavens. "There are some things with which I really have trouble. Washing your son in camel urine is one!"

Joseph laughed, then continued brushing sand off the donkey. Presently a man appeared, wrapped in his abbah and head-cloth, hiding everything except sparkling eyes and a bushy beard. Waving a dagger, he shouted, "The sheik would like to see all of you! Follow me!"

Quickly, Mary picked up Jesus from the basket, took Joseph's arm and followed the man. As the dove swooped toward Joseph's shoulder, the man jumped up and took a spread stance as though he were going to whack the bird in two with his weapon. "No! No!" shouted Joseph, arms waving. "She's our pet!"

"Oh," grunted the man, acting disappointed. "They are a delicacy to a Bedouin." He looked heavenward, and smacked his lips with his fingertips, closing his eyes, remembering a moment of bliss. "Ah, yes! Keep an eye on her." He winked at Mary and continued trudging toward a large tent. Joseph raised his eyebrows toward Mary and shrugged his shoulders.

Sand swirled around them as they approached the tent. The structure stood half its height, being put up in a hurry the previous night. The man pulled the tarp flap back while Mary and Joseph ducked, stepping inside. The ceiling barely touched Joseph's head.

"Come inside, Joseph and Mary of Nazareth!" bellowed a man sitting crosslegged on a carpet, sipping from a goblet. He was a huge man, gray hair sprouting in every direction under his turban. One look and Joseph thought, "I should like to be on good terms with this one." Next to the man perched a large black hawk on a T pole that stuck in the sand. The hawk paced nervously after spying the dove on Joseph. He lowered his head, eyes glaring, and arched his great wings. Fearing this predator, the dove ducked under Joseph's hair on his neck. Grunting, the big man reached over and pulled a hood over the hawk's head. The hawk stood still.

"Sit down! Please!" The bronze hand, decked in rings, pointed to ornamental cushions. Mary and Joseph nodded, as was custom to a sheik of the desert, then seated themselves crosslegged. Mary propped Jesus on her lap. Silently, the big man searched his visitors' faces. The wind bumped the walls of the tent like a pounding fist.

"I am Bon Ami, son of Phanuel, son of Anizah, son of Shararat, son of Ishmael, son of Abraham and Hagar. Welcome to my tent."

Bon Ami stretched his hands forward. "May I see the child?" Joseph took Jesus from Mary, handing Him over to the sheik.

"So this is the boy that is causing the great furor with Herod," roared Bon Ami. Joseph darted a glance at Mary. She returned the look. How did he know?

Without looking up, still searching the baby's face, Bon Ami responded, "Word travels quickly among the faithful." Joseph and Mary looked questioningly. Bon Ami continued to gaze peacefully into Jesus' face. "Joseph and Mary of Nazareth, you do not think that after waiting years and years for the Messiah, knowing He is now among us, that we would let Him slip away so easily?" Bon Ami sat quietly for a moment, still studying Jesus.

"My very old sister is Anna, the prophetess, the old woman who saw and recognized Jesus at the temple in Jerusalem. From that day she has been dragging her ancient frame preaching among the women about Jesus.

"The Magi of the East sent a scout seeking the location of the caravan with which you might join. He left desert supplies: a small tent, dried food, and water skins." Mary sighed and concealed a secret smile concerning the water. "I have waited with my desert caravan loaded with tribesmen to pick you up. We had a man staked out at the well to notify us of your arrival. We couldn't leave your lives in the hands of any caravan coming through. Thieving and raiding run rampant on these routes. Herod, even now, has his soldiers scouting this area."

Bon Ami handed Jesus back to Mary. "The journey will be long and hot. We should have no problems with attacks. I have a powerful caravan with the best fighters on the Egyptian routes."

Bon Ami faced Joseph. "I understand you are a carpenter, Joseph?" Joseph nodded. "We can use you with saddle and various repairs."

"Mary and I would be glad to help in any way we can."

"Thank you, Joseph. Now I can report back to Anna. She, in return, can report your safety to others."

The men clasped arms in friendship, and Mary and Joseph took their leave. Mary threaded her arm through Joseph's. She pulled him to a stop, looking up with grateful eyes.

"Just when you think you are alone and the journey seems hopeless, love keeps popping up and inches you step by step through the impossibility of it all. It is incredible what we have been through, but here we are." The wind rippled her mantle, her beautiful face becoming distant. "I'm sure we have more to go through. But, knowing God is with us, I will accept all things gracefully, even though I don't understand. God has a greater purpose for all this which we cannot see. In the end, all this will work together for good."

Postscript

❄

Overall, the trip to Egypt was enjoyable for the Holy Family. Once they reached Memphis, Mary and Joseph took leave of Bon Ami and their caravan friends. They secured a peasant dwelling in a small village in the Nile Delta. With the provisions that Bon Ami left, they set up housekeeping. Joseph took up carpentry and Mary wove baskets from the reeds of the river. They bartered these goods for daily food and supplies.

Jesus napped or played on a blanket at Mary's feet while she worked. The boy and the bird were inseparable. Jesus crawled everywhere and the dove waited upon His every wish.

At three years Jesus spoke fluent Hebrew and exercised continual questions and conversations with His bird. Often sitting in front of the flat-roofed house, he pointed out various insects, clouds, or other things of nature. The dove attended to every word. As Jesus grew stronger in boyhood, the dove grew weaker with age. She didn't take long flights to the skies any more and her once-mangled wing ached. She began spending more time perched on a window ledge bathing in the warm sunlight. In the yard she watched Joseph teach Jesus how to hammer nails, saw boards, and polish wood with oils.

The dove still cooed the boy a lullaby at dusk but this also tired her. Faithfully, every night she nestled upon his pillow above curly hair, tucked her head under wing, and dreamed of soaring high among the clouds.

One morning Mary came upon the dove sitting listless near a door. Jesus gently picked up his pet and found the rocking chair that Joseph had made for him. Gathering around, the family touched and spoke loving words to this small being that brought so much love to their lives. Inevitably, the dove had to say goodbye in a sorrowful, almost inaudible, last song.

Jesus didn't leave her side. He knew where she was going. In spite of who He was and what He knew, in His childlike humanness, He experienced His first earthly bereavement, a tearing, a ripping away. She was leaving Him. This grief seeded the understanding of things to come.

As the sun rose one morning, Mary and Joseph found Jesus sitting crosslegged in bed with streaming tears. To His breast He lovingly held the limp form of His beloved white dove.

Postscript 2

❋

The dove awoke, feeling a strange, drawing sensation. At the time her small body, cold and lifeless, felt more pain than she could endure.

Suddenly she felt herself pulled upward — so light, so free, so wonderful, translucent but still in the form of a dove. Casting a glance downward, she saw her old self still curled in the sleeping child's hands. The form, ashen and still, was the shell of her discarded body.

She spiraled upward faster and faster as though a great magnet of light pulled her away from the earth. She was somewhat frightened, yet elated, for an eagle could go no faster.

She crossed through a brilliant chasm, coming to a golden gate that seemed bigger than life. The mighty portals automatically opened and she flew through into a beautiful world.

This world revealed rivers, woods, seas, and mountains filled with nature's spirits such as herself. Deer, gazelles, lions, sheep, rabbits, butterflies, birds, and every imaginable creature of the animal kingdom dwelled within. A lion grazed with a sheep and a wolf sunned himself next to a fawn.

The dove thought, "This is far more beautiful than the best of the earthly world." She sailed about, saw the sharpened colors, smelled true sweetness, and heard the full sounds of pure creation. Birds sang, crickets chirped, the breeze rustled, and richness of life prevailed as the dove had never experienced it before. Everything looked, sounded, and smelled as if it were intended and meant for so much more.

She flew over a bubbling brook. Intense thirst pulled her toward it. Perched on a rock, she thrust her bill deeply into the stream, drinking the sparkling water, pure and cold. She was energized forever.

Lifting a dripping beak, she noticed human beings of every race, tribe, nation, and language. Men, women, children, and babies in angels' arms dipped from the stream, then walked slowly in the same direction, moving toward a huge golden city.

The city, big as the universe itself, was surrounded by walls made of an element resembling gold, but unblemished and more vitalized.

The dove flew through an enormous archway leading into the city. The city, animated with workers, radiated the fullness of life. People walked or floated about their business. Artists chiseled intricate symbols in the city walls, painters painted figures around stained glass windows. Tradesmen worked in immaculate buildings, and through the windows the dove saw some studying books, some drawing architectural designs, some working machines, some researching, and some discoursing in deep discussion. People came and went with excitement and urgency. Countless souls traveled through the entrance gate, leaving the golden city at great speeds to distances beyond the mountains.

Flying farther into the city, the dove heard the most extraordinary chorus of human voices. The great choir swelled, praising and rejoicing. Listening, she experienced the greatest expression of love in sound she had ever heard.

Farther on, an orchestra played, pulsing the heartbeat of the Kingdom. Every note sounded pure, natural, blessed. The harmony blended every good and beautiful thing.

As she continued, she saw dancers dancing, teachers teaching, chemists experimenting, doctors theorizing, children playing. Each person exuberated such drive and joy that it brought beauty and perfection to the magnificent city.

A large seven-foot archangel swooped close to the dove, a finger reaching forward. The white-robed woman, older than most angels, had a jovial grin, twinkling eyes, and white curly hair. Angels such as she were assigned to each creature entering the city, leading each to assignments throughout the Kingdom.

Unhesitatingly, the bird hopped on the guardian angel's finger, communicating easily with this happy being. Hardly making a noise, they read each other's minds perfectly. The angel said, "Come with me, beautiful one. God would like to see you."

The dove thought of all the times Jesus spoke of His Father in heaven. Many times she had felt God's presence of holy light. But now! Meet God face to face? She trembled.

Together the dove and the angel entered a golden portal of mystical light surrounded by thousands of archangels, heralding trumpets.

The throne of God lay ahead. At first, the brilliance and glowing splendor blinded the dove. Slowly her eyes adjusted to the aura. Her guardian angel landed, stopping upon a silver carpet. She spoke sofly, reverently. "You will have to fly forward yourself to stand before God." With a wave of her hand, she released the bird.

Small heart pounding, the white dove fluttered straight into dazzling glory, surrounded by hues of a rainbow. The light bathed her in warmth, love, and understanding. She knew everything she had heard about a loving, kind Father was true. Fear and trembling were replaced with peace and joy.

She settled at the foot of the throne, not seeing through the radiance, but feeling the loving warmth of the great Being before her. So tiny and fragile, silently she stood waiting for God to speak. God's voice was as fine and rich as the four seasons of earth at their best.

"You pleased me, little friend. You served My Son well. Every soul that faithfully loves, no matter how small that life may be, furthers My Kingdom. You nurtured My Child and are very dear to His heart. Steadfastly you stood by His side. Thank you."

There was a long pause. Then God asked, "How would you like to see Jesus again?"

The white dove exploded with happiness and lost her balance, falling backwards while peeking out from under a wing. God's laughter thundered throughout the universe. The dove found her happy spirit joining His. The laughter ceased. God spoke again. "When Jesus begins His holy order,

I would like to celebrate this special event. At His baptism, I have selected you to carry the Holy Spirit to Him, demonstrating to the world My special blessings. Are you willing to do this for Me?" Without hesitation the white dove eagerly communicated yes.

When the time came, the Almighty God cradled the white dove in palms of brilliant light. He gently lifted her. The Holy Spirit circled her like a sparkling cape. Billions of angels gathered like billowing clouds as the omnipotent arms of God parted the heavens. With the glory of the world looking upon her, the white dove descended from the ages.

The white wings soared downward. There was no limit to what this new body could do. She swung into the wind, bright tips outstretched, coming closer to Jesus. Her eyes strained to see Him clearly. The feeling of glory and joyousness blended with euphoria in coming back to Him. He knew her. He held out his hands in the same old way. He looked older, taller, wiser, but the stance, the eyes, and the smile were the same.

She flew to Him, alighting on His shoulder, the feel familiar. Their joy knew no bounds in the re-uniting. The powerful Holy Spirit left the dove, remaining in Christ's body.

The proud voice of God the Father came down from heaven, ringing out to all the corners of the world. "This is my beloved Son, in whom I am well pleased."

The dove stayed with her Master, and remains with Him today. Her appearances with him, or representing him, are endless. She, a mere dove, was chosen to represent the Unseen Spirit. Wherever you go on earth, in all walks of life, in all places, the dove reminds us that we are not alone.

❄

The Spirit soars where love prevails,
Beholding the eye of your soul.

She glides like a dove with soft, white wings,
To reach His Immortal goal.

Fly with her light, mount and sail,
Aloft, she carries you far.

And in the end, God leads you both,
To where the blessed are.

❄